SHADOWS
AND
DECEPTION

Shadows and Deception

ISBN 13: 979-8-9914240-0-4

ISBN 13: 979-8-9914240-1-1

ISBN 13: 979-8-9914240-2-8

First Edition: September 2024

www.cjmckinney.com

Trigger Warning: For a full list of trigger warnings, please visit www.cjmckinney.com.

SHADOWS AND DECEPTION

CJ MCKINNEY

"The truth is this, every monster you have met, was once a human being with a soul that was as soft and light as silk. Someone stole that silk from their soul and turned them into this. So, when you see a monster next, always remember this. Do not fear the thing before you. Fear the thing that created it instead."

-Nikita Gill

Chapter One
Ghost

Walking through the door, screaming soothes my ears as I eagerly make my way downstairs to see what fun awaits today. Don't worry, nobody will ever know about this place. They won't ever hear the screams, the pain, the begging. A grin spreads across my face as the cold metal door creaks open. The muggy basement greets me as the faint smell of death assaults my nose.

Smirking when I hear, "It's about time you showed up."

Taking in the scene before me, Ace, Luke, and Cam are all hanging around like it's just another day. My best friend, Ace, is a lot more twisted than I am, which is saying a lot. He's standing there holding a knife that's somehow glimmering, even with blood dripping on the floor.

Damn, hopefully that won't stain.

Who am I kidding? The man hanging from the metal pipe is more than dripping.

Luke is leaning against the wall, arms crossed, chewing on a toothpick looking a little less than excited. His chestnut-colored hair hangs across his forehead as he stares daggers at the man before us. Convinced, he believes that if he smiles, his face will break. Cam is standing to his left, animatedly telling him about a puppy he had seen on the sidewalk earlier today. With his blonde hair, green eyes, and unmatched energy, you can tell he still has some hope for the world. Good. It means we protected him- more than we protected ourselves.

Walking over, examining his handy work, the unlucky soul stares back at me through an already swollen eye.

His moans are barely audible.

"Did you find anything on him?" My eyes meet Luke and Cam's.

Cam pipes up, "Yeah, we were able to find him on a security camera at an old run down gas station walking with a scrawny kid, probably in his 20s. This guy's name happens to be Cade."

Leaning down to meet "Cade's" deathly stare, "Did you learn your lesson?"

He spits in my face and grins. Red covers my vision as my body tenses. Grabbing the rag from Ace's table of toys, the rough fabric pulls at my skin as it cleans off the filth.

Smiling back and nodding at Ace, "Finish him."

A wave of exhaustion overwhelms me when the chill of the air blows against my face. Walking straight to my car, my fingers fire off a message to the boys to let them know to take the night off after cleaning up. Backing up, the decision to take the long way back to the city is evident.

I need fresh air. Desperately.

Luckily, every red light on the way back is green until one. Looking to my right, the silhouette of a man standing against the brick wall is barely visible in the darkness. Squinting my eyes, noticing it's the same man we saw hanging around our most recent visitor, Cade. Pulling over and throwing the car in park. Instinctively, my hand goes to the gun on my hip. He runs.

Shocker.

He disappears into the alley before my hands can wrap around his throat. A rat scurries across my path as I put one foot in front of the other, attempting to avoid the puddles. Taking turn after turn, the main road comes back into view, with him nowhere in sight.

"Motherfucker," I mumble.

Leaning against the brick wall, the cool air burns my lungs.

3

Ringing fills my ears in the dead of night. Calling Ace, it goes straight to voicemail.

Of course.

"Call me back, it's important," I bark out.

Steadying my breathing, my eyes close, bracing for the adrenaline crash.

The vacant streets don't whisper a sound apart from the sirens in the distance and the faint music in the bar across the street.

God, they have terrible taste.

A sign that says *The Hideaway* dimly lights the sidewalk. Wall-to-wall windows allow a glimpse inside to see people mingling around a pool table, filling the air with smoke. Despite the scene before me, most of the city is asleep. The streetlamp flickers off in the distance.

My face sports a permanent scowl until my eyes land on her. A look of surprise appears, but quickly brushing it off, my focus returns to her. She's walking to her car from the bar, laughing with a friend. Relaxed, like nothing could bother her. Dark brown hair swings as she throws her head back, laughing. Undoubtedly, it is the most perfect sound that's ever met my ears.

No, this can't happen.

Despite the urge to turn away, something about her keeps my eyes glued to her. A wave of protectiveness pours over me like hot lava- a need to keep her safe.

Away from people like me.

At that moment, my eyes snap to a man walking behind her. Rage flows through my veins, realizing it's the man from the alley.

4

His focus is narrowed on what's mine. My steps are light, unlike the shadows that engulf me. He doesn't register my presence behind him. My hand wraps around his mouth, dragging him quickly back to my place in the darkness. His back hits the brick wall.

Removing my hand from his mouth, he attempts to spit out, "What the fu-"

My fist connects with his nose, causing his skull to slam against the wall. The cracking sound echoes in the silence. Unable to stop, my fist continues over and over until his lifeless body drops at my feet.

I'm not good for her.

Despite my internal protesting, my feet take me back to where I was before. Studying her even as blood drips from my hands. Thankfully, she isn't the one driving tonight, seeing as she almost missed the car seat when getting in. Watching as she slams the door, the car roars to life. Taillights disappear into the night.

I'll find her.

As soon as the thought passes, my phone vibrates. Groaning as my finger hesitates to answer when Ace's name isn't the one on the screen.

"What is it now?" I bark into the phone.

My brother-in-law, River, laughs, "I need you to take down the attitude first. But since you're so happy to hear from me, I just called to invite you to dinner tomorrow evening."

Rolling my eyes to the point they very well may get stuck in that position, "You do know how to brighten my day, asshole. I'll be there."

Spotting my car, that thankfully wasn't towed, a sigh escapes my lips. Sliding in, my head rests against the seat, the blood forgotten. Reluctantly, I decide to make my way back to the place I call home- for now.

Looking up at the two-story house as my hand reaches the gate. A deep gray color coats the siding as black shutters sit next to the windows. A matching waisthigh iron gate surrounds the yard, paired with two giant oak trees in the front, keeping the neighbors wondering what's behind them. Stepping onto the porch, creaking with each step, the keys nearly slip through my fingers. Just enough moonlight lights up the night to give me the ability to make out the doorknob. My foot lifts to step inside just in time to see my life flash before my eyes.

That damn rug needs to go.

The patter of my little angel fills my ears before she comes into view. All ten pounds of fluff. While my reputation precedes me, she is, admittedly, my soft spot. Quickly scooping her up, we make our way to the kitchen. After filling up her bowl, the raid on the refrigerator results in nothing to eat except leftovers.

So many options- not.

Grabbing the take-out box and placing it in the microwave, my fingers tap on the counter as the timer counts down. My shoulders relax ever so slightly. Unable to remember the last time that happened, my shoulders begin to tense again.

Such a shame.

My mind wanders back to her. Seemingly free as a bird- my little bird. Jumping as the microwave beeps, the noise pulls me out of my thoughts as steam warms my face. Making my way to the couch only to find Snowball asleep under a blanket. Trust me, the name was not my idea. I adopted her from a pound three years ago, and now she rules the house.

Well, I guess I'll take the chair then.

The TV comes to life, and it soon becomes nothing but background noise. Not a single word from the reporter's mouth sticks. My mind only seems to be thinking of one thing. Her. Perfect curves complement her petite frame, topped with a smile that would bring a man to his knees. Towering over most people as a mountain of a man, the image of her beside me is unavoidable. To have her run her fingers through my hair and those soft, pink lips on mine. The things I would do.

One day.

SHADOWS AND DECEPTION

Chapter Two
Rain

My head is pounding. The light coming in through the blinds is shining directly through my eyelids. Eyes still screwed shut, my hand runs over the nightstand for a glass of water.

Of course, it's not there.

Peeling myself out of bed and into the kitchen, the glass fumbles in my hand, nearly shattering on the floor. Filling it to the brim, the cool liquid coats my throat. Now fully awake, the smell of alcohol from my pores invades my nose. Peeling off the clothes that stick to my skin, I gracefully toss them into the basket.

SHADOWS AND DECEPTION

Okay, I may have missed it.

Stepping into the shower, the scorching water hits my skin, relaxing every muscle. Grabbing the half-empty shampoo bottle, squeezing a quarter-size amount into my palm, it lathers as my fingers massage my scalp. The coarse sensation of the loofa meets my skin as soap bubbles. The distinct vanilla scent meets the air. Closing my eyes, the man from the darkness enters my mind. The streetlamp barely hit his face. I don't think he realized I saw him. Cassi interrupted my thoughts of the man rambling about some guy from inside the bar. Apparently, he was beyond drunk, had two left feet, and nearly threw up on her shoes, causing us both to erupt into a fit of laughter. After she finally unlocked the door, almost missing my seat, she triggered another round of laughter. Closing the car door, I glanced back one last time. He was still staring. I decided then, I wanted a closer look at the man in the shadows.

Once the water turns to ice, a fluffy towel wraps around me. My hair decides for me that a ponytail is the only answer for today as it chooses to look like a bird's nest. Yanking the dresser drawer open and shoving half the clothes aside, my hand meets a set of gray scrubs. Hopping from foot to foot, focusing on not losing my balance, my socks slip on without me landing on my face. Pulling the pantry door open, my face turns down in a frown. It's about a day away from having cobwebs. There's one single snack bar in the back corner. Heading out the door, my hand snatches the water bottle and the stale snack bar.

As my hands reach for the car door, the noise of my phone ringing pierces through my skull. Balancing everything in one arm,

I snatch my phone out of my pocket, wedging it between my cheek and shoulder. "Hey girl, I was just calling to check and see how you are doing this fine morning," Cassi says, amusement laced in her tone.

"I'm perfectly fine, thank you very much, but tell me, how are your shoes doing?" chuckling, remembering last night.

She groans, "I already told you he missed when he used them as target practice for throwing up. Ugh, don't make me think about that anymore. It was traumatizing."

"Trust me, you told me all about it," rolling my eyes. "Hey, you know I could always ask the girls from work to come with us."

Sobering, "You know my past, Cass. I have to go to work. I'll talk to you later. Love you!"

"I love you too. You better be safe." The call ends with one last look in the rear-view mirror before backing out.

Let me say working as a nurse in an emergency room with a hangover is the opposite of a good time. Shifting the car into park after finding an empty parking spot in the overfilled lot, my eyes close as a deep breath enters my lungs.

Relax.

Attempting to make it to the breakroom, screaming and crying from the lobby overwhelms my senses.

I should've stayed in bed.

The beeping of the time clock fills my ears. Rounding the corner, my eyes search for another nurse.

A small, red-faced man comes into my line of sight, shrieking because his stubbed toe hasn't been seen in a timely manner," Why have I not been seen yet? I've been here for over ten minutes! My toe hurts!"

"Go have a seat, please; they will see you shortly," forcing a smile.

My eyes land on a young girl around my age curled up in a chair. Short blonde hair covers her face. Her arms wrapped tightly around her legs, making her appear smaller than she is. Her brows are drawn together as she stares into space. Turning away from the chaos, my eyes land on Maggie. She runs a hand over her hair, which is slowly falling out of the braid she had it in. Dark circles under her eyes give away just how exhausted she is.

A wide grin covers her face as her eyes regain a small amount of sparkle. "Thank goodness you're here. I can't handle anymore today," letting out a sigh.

"Give me the short version and get out of here. I know you need the rest," giving her a soft smile.

She skims over what her shift was like. Eyes wide and mouth parted, wondering if calling in was the better option. Processing everything she said, she's up and bouncing out the door.

I hope she remembered to clock out.

Beeping assaults my ears, never letting up as the wailing continues. As soon as we get one person out of here, five more appear.

Send help.

Chapter Three

Ghost

Tossing and turning all night made sleep my enemy. Making the difficult decision to peel myself out of bed, the sunlight begins to shine in through the smudged window. Pulling on my sweatpants, the morning air hits my skin. Walking downstairs, the hardwood floor freezes my toes. While grabbing a coffee mug, my finger meets the glowing button on the machine.

The one thing that makes mornings a little more bearable.

Soon, the smell of coffee takes over the entire house. Making my way to the front porch, the old wooden rocking chair creaks under my weight, too lost in my thoughts to care. My brows draw together, wondering just how I'll be able to see her again. My phone rings, bringing me back to reality.

"Good morning, dear!" River sings.

It is way too early for this.

"What could you possibly want? The sun is barely up."

"Well, since you asked so nicely, I have a job." The seriousness in his voice makes my spine straighten.

"Okay, shoot."

He laughs again, "That's exactly what you'll be doing."

Oh shit.

"Fucker's been drugging girls at The Hideaway. They've been waking up on sidewalks or in hospitals and remember little to nothing."

My heart drops not only for those women but the fact that my woman was there last night.

My woman?

Shaking it off, "Text me the details. I got it."

"Thanks, man." The call ends.

Deciding to slip on my shoes as my blood boils. My shoes meet the pavement. Every step dissolves the anger inside of me. The sun is barely over the horizon, birds chirping fills the silence as people leave for work. An hour later, my feet drag against each porch step as sweat trails down my body, signaling the desperate need for a shower.

Slipping off my shoes by the door, my feet drag up the stairs. Grabbing a soft towel as my pants fall to the floor, the faucet squeaks as the water begins flowing, steaming up the mirror. The freezing droplets hit my skin. Closing my eyes, my head falls forward, resting on the black tile.

One look at her, and I'm about to burn the world down. I'll set myself on fire if that's what it takes to keep her safe.

My head pulls back from the tile as shampoo works through my hair. The earthy scent fills the bathroom. The faucet squeaks again as it turns off. Drying off with the towel from the towel rack, it wraps around my waist. My feet pad across the room into the walk-in closet, warm light glows throughout. Pulling a shirt off the clothes hanger and jeans from the dresser below, they slip over my damp body.

Jogging back downstairs, I shove my feet into an old pair of scuffed boots. Leaning down to pet Snowball, she rolls on her back expecting belly scratches, which she, of course, gets. The door slams behind me. Getting in the car, the windows immediately roll down. My trip to Ace's begins with the breeze blowing through my hair. The front of his house comes into view as the front door swings open. His face is back into a scowl that matches mine. Believe it or not, he is most certainly *not* a morning person. He holds a cup of coffee out, knowing it's exactly what we'll both need. Fully aware my first cup has completely worn off the warm liquid meets my lips. Filling him in on the fact someone has been drugging women at The Hideaway, leaving out a tiny detail that includes my new obsession, he goes over what River sent as his grip on my phone slowly tightens. Apparently, this guy, who we found out was Cade, is only one part of the puzzle. He's the fall

15

guy. He and his partner go in, manipulate, and somehow gets them in his car, meeting up with someone afterward. We aren't sure who just yet, but luckily, River got us an address for the unlucky guy.

Pulling up in front of what looks like an abandoned house, we take in the disaster. There is no way someone lives here- the screen door barely hangs on, one window is busted, paired with a rotted porch that may or may not hold our weight. As we cautiously step up, we listen for any sound of movement. The faint sound of a TV is barely audible. Moving to the window, Ace shakes his head. He can't see anything through the blinds. Moving over to the busted-out window, attempting to avoid shards of glass, a horrific smell invades my nose. There's still no sign of him.

Nodding as we draw our guns, Ace splinters the door in one swift movement. Moldy food and empty wrappers litter the kitchen. The living room doesn't look much better, with beer bottles, cigarette ashes, and cockroaches blanketing every surface. Chipped paint covers the door directly in front of us. Busting through that door, a wave of nausea hits.

A man who has to be in his 20s lies on a stained mattress passed out. Needles and more empty alcohol bottles surround him. Taking a step forward, nudging him with my boot, he doesn't move. There's still a chance we can get answers, seeing that his chest is still moving. Ace moves from behind me with his arm over his nose.

"Let's get him out of here-" Before the sentence can come out, a bullet rips through my leg.

I guess he wasn't passed out.

He lets out a scream as Ace puts a bullet through his foot. Knocking the gun out of his hand and ignoring my pain, his arm twists in an unnatural position, which makes flipping him over easy.

"You move the wrong way, and it's going to snap like a twig. Today's your lucky day. You get to go join your buddy." Turning around to see Ace's face in a maniacal smile, he helps me haul him up. A faded leather wallet lies on the floor.

Jackpot.

He has a solid three dollars and his ID.

Tyler.

Well, Tyler, did your boss warn you about this part of the job? Dragging him around the car, we toss him in the trunk. He'll be fine- for now. It looks like that metal pipe has another unfortunate guest.

SHADOWS AND DECEPTION

Chapter Four

Rain

"Motherfucker," I hiss. Feeling my lip, blood covers my fingertips. It's been one hell of a night seeing as how a patient coming down from a high tried to deck me in the face. Luckily, I dodged, or I would've ended up in here myself.

"Rain! Get out here."

So, help me if one more thing happens.

I walk out to my manager, Debbie, tapping her foot with her arms folded across her chest looking a little less than happy. "We have another patient and everyone else is busy."

Forcing a smile, "I got it."

Looking down her nose, she nods and walks off.

Thanks for the help.

I walk into the exam room and stop in my tracks.

Well, this just got interesting.

I'm met with the man I can't seem to stop thinking about. His piercing gaze meets mine. Eyes so blue they're nearly silver stare back at me. Black hair hangs over his forehead like he's been running his hands through it. Surprise is written all over his face.

Stepping up to him, "I'm Rain, now what seems to be going on?"

Breaking the connection, my eyes drift down to his leg. My eyes nearly pop out of my head. I see blood- a lot of blood.

Grabbing a pair of gloves and gauze out of the drawer, I go back and start putting pressure on the bullet wound. His eyes never leave me. It won't stop bleeding.

Other nurses and doctors begin running in. I go to pull away when he grabs my wrist.

"What happened?" as he brushes his thumb over the split in my lip.

I lean back, "It's no big deal. The question is what happened to you?"

The corner of his mouth turns up, "It's no big deal."

I'm fascinated by him, but instantly notice how pale he's becoming. The next thing I know he's being wheeled out of the room and heading to the OR leaving me gaping as the room empties. Turning around, I see a giant man wide eyed staring past me. I gently touch his arm bringing him back to the world around us.

"Is he going to be alright?" worry covers his face. "He'll be just fine." giving him a soft smile.

I hope.

Cleaning up from the chaos that just happened, I hear him begin, "I had to pretty much drag Ghost in here. The guy will be on his deathbed saying he's fine. By the way, I'm Ace."

Ghost?

He must have seen the confusion on my face.

"That's what he goes by. He doesn't answer to anything else." He walks toward the hallway barely turning back, "I have to make a phone call. I'll be up in the waiting room after." Not waiting for an answer, he walks away.

Hours go by with "Ghost" still in surgery. With everything happening so fast, I was unable to look at his name on the chart. Thankfully, I finish the rest of my shift somehow in one piece.

Walking to the waiting room to check for any updates on his condition, I'm met with Ace's big form taking up one of the small chairs meant for a normal sized human. His hat covers his eyes, arms folded, and head down. I quietly take a seat on the couch closest to him unable to keep from fidgeting with the hem of my top while thoughts begin racing through my mind.

What could be taking so long? Is something wrong? Why the hell do I care? I don't even know his real name.

The double doors finally open. Ace's head darts up looking around, eyes soften when they land on me. I stand and walk towards the white-headed man who introduces himself as the surgeon. He proceeds to explain there was a significant amount of blood loss, but surgery went well, and he will overall be just fine. With a sigh of relief from both of us, I step up asking when we will be able to see him. He informs us he will need to stay overnight to see how he does. Ace lets out a chuckle under his breath. I glance over as he's shaking his head. The doctor ignores him as he gives us the room number. Turning, we begin walking towards the elevator to make our way upstairs.

"He is not going to be happy," he mumbles to himself.

Rocking back and forth on my feet, I let out a breath when the elevator finally dings, signaling we're on our floor. I exit first and walk up to the nurses' desk where a middle-aged woman looks like she's ready to go home already.

"Hey, Kate."

"Hey, Rain, it's been a while since I've seen you up here. Sorry it's been crazy."

"You're telling me. Hey, I have a friend up here. Do you think you could let the no visitor thing slide tonight?"

"I didn't see that he had visitors and won't be checking for any for a while." She sends us off with a wink.

Standing by the door, I feel incredibly awkward since I don't really know the man lying in the hospital bed. Ace nudges me forward, but as I raise my foot to take a step through the door, the elevator dings with a frantic looking young man stepping out as his green eyes dart in every direction. A second man appears behind him with a scowl that attempts to hide the fear that's clearly present.

Ace bends down whispering, "The crazed looking one is Cam, and the grouchy one is Luke."

Cam runs past the desk completely ignoring poor Kate. He walks right into the room taking a seat on the couch while I slowly walk in taking the last open seat by the head of the bed. Looking over, Ace stands by the foot of the bed taking in the tubes and wires as Luke stands in the doorway hesitant to come in.

Looking down at the man in front of us, I take him in. He looks a lot better compared to when I last saw him. The color has returned to his skin.

Cam breaks the silence, "What the hell happened man?"

Rolling his eyes, "It's just a scratch. I'm fine."

I can't help but scoff at his response, "You most certainly are not fine seeing as how you are currently laying in a hospital bed," His eyes meet mine, surprised by my response. "What?! It's true, and you know it."

Luke pipes in, "She has a valid point."

Crossing my arms across my chest, "See? I told you."

"Since when did you two join forces? This one's bad enough on his own," crossing his arms to match mine.

Kate interrupts when she knocks on the door, poking her head inside. She continues to come in multiple times to check on all of us. Dozing off, the feeling of something under my hand gains my attention. My eyes snap open, looking down. His fingers are rubbing circles over my skin.

Lifting my eyes to meet his, "Hey, little bird."

Ignoring the confusion written on my face, "What made you decide to come check on me?".

My brain decides that's the perfect moment to stop functioning, "Um... well, I- I just wanted to see how you were doing after I saw the shape you were in downstairs."

A smug look takes over his face, "So you come to sit with all your patients and their best friends?"

Glancing over, Ace and Cam sit on opposite sides of the couch asleep.

Luke sits in a single chair in the corner with his nose in his phone until he abruptly stands, "I'm going to grab some coffee, I'll be right back." I nod as he walks out the door.

Looking back at him, "Well, no."

His face grows into a full grin, but he quickly winces. Standing to go get Kate, he grabs my hand, "Don't go. Please." His brows draw together.

He draws his hand back as if it was on fire.

Ignoring the feeling in my chest, "Let me go get her first. I'll be right back."

Hearing a scream come from the end of a hall, Kate walks out, shaking her head. We go back into Ghost's room where he's attempting to sit up to get out of bed. Rushing over, my hands land on his chest, gently pushing him back.

"What the hell do you think you're doing?" raising one eyebrow at him.

"Well, I came to the realization, again, that I am perfectly fine, and I'm going home."

"No, just no. Sit your ass back and let us take care of you."

"Fine."

He has the audacity to pout like a child, which immediately earns an eye roll. After Kate finishes up, we're left alone. His eyes burn into the side of my face while I attempt to avoid his gaze. The door opens as he opens his mouth to speak, revealing Luke holding two coffee cups. He walks over and shoves one in my hand.

"Thank you," giving him a soft smile.

He grumbles as he returns to his spot. An older man in a white coat walks in, looking from the glasses at the end of his nose to Ghost, "Good news. Everything looked great throughout the night, so you'll be able to be discharged today on one condition. You must have someone to help with your daily activities. You can't put your full weight on that leg just yet. I'll let the nurse know." He turns and walks out before we can ask any questions.

Ghost groans. With my eyebrows drawn, the lack of pure joy at the news confuses me. "Do you have an extra room, Ace?"

Ace hesitates, looking between us. "You can always stay, but I have two kids running around. I doubt you would get any rest."

Luke joins in, "I have some things going on, so I won't be home to help."

"Same here. Sorry, man," Cam says without an ounce of remorse.

Immediately making eye contact with Ace, his face doesn't give anything away.

Closing his eyes, he takes a deep breath. Taking that as a sign he doesn't have anyone else that he's close enough to stay with, if any at all.

He could stay at home. That wouldn't be a complete disaster, would it? Probably.

"I have room if you need a place to stay." The words leave my mouth before my brain can catch up.

He stares at me in disbelief, as if he can't believe I just said that. Honestly, I can't blame him, neither can I.

"That would be way too much for you. Why would you want a stranger staying with you anyway?"

He has a valid point.

"You're not going to murder me in my sleep, are you? Or be all creepy?"

Everyone lets out a laugh as he rolls his eyes. "That's not normally on my agenda."

"There we go. Anything weird, and you'll be shipped off to one of these guys. Deal?"

"Deal." He finally relaxes back.

Chapter Five

Ghost

That did not just happen.

From the wink Ace threw my way when Rain wasn't looking, I knew exactly what he was doing. A word hasn't been uttered about the night in the alley to him or anyone else.

This is a terrible idea.

I should just tell her that Ace's will be fine, but for some reason, the words won't come out, and it's not because of the lack of sleep I would be getting.

Raising up, a shooting pain runs through my leg. I have to get out of here. One of the guys brought me a set of clean clothes last night, hence the bag landing at the foot of the bed.

"Do you need help?" Luke nods at the bag.

"No, I've got it, but thanks. You can head home. I'll let you know when I get to Rain's place."

Ace pauses, "I'll send you an update on the- situation," and heads toward the door.

As they walk out, standing sends another shock of pain up my leg. The no-weight thing clearly slipped my mind.

"Shit!" collapsing back on the bed.

"Are you okay? Here, let me help." Rain looks at me with those brown that that remind me of honey, changing from puzzled to alarmed. Unaware that she has been watching me the entire time.

"I'm fine. I can get it."

"No. Stop being stubborn and stay right there."

This is going to be fun.

She reaches over, unzipping my bag, and bends down as a wave of vanilla hits my nose.

Calm down, Ghost. You can't let her get close to you. Someone gets hurt. Every. Time.

Slowly raising each leg, she slides my sweatpants on keeping her head turned and her body tense. Putting my weight on my good leg, she helps me stand. They slide up as the cotton brushes against my bandages. Pulling off the hospital gown to put my shirt on, her eyes widen as they stare at my chest, working their way down. Clearing my throat, she jumps and shakes her head.

"Sorry, here," shoving my shirt into my hands.

She walks out the door to hunt down a nurse for my discharge paperwork and a wheelchair. Despite my protesting, she comes back to the room with both.

Tapping brings me out of a trance when her foot catches my attention. Apparently, we're both ready to leave. After what seems like forever, the elevator finally dings. Quickly hitting the button, we're left standing in silence as elevator music plays.

I'm going to kill the guy that shot me.

Rubbing the back of my neck, "Thank you for letting me stay for a bit. I'll be out of your hair as soon as I can."

"It's really no problem. You can stay as long as you need to."

Silence covers us once again. We're able to make our way through the lobby into the parking lot, breathing in fresh air, reality comes back into frame. The man responsible for this mess instantly makes another appearance in my mind. The text to Ace immediately asks for an update, despite knowing he most likely doesn't have one, seeing as how he just left the hospital.

Rain hands me her phone as she continues pushing the wheelchair, "Here, put your number in there in case I need to get ahold of you."

I send myself a quick message, so I have her number too— you know, in case of an actual emergency. I return it to her, and she slips it back into the front pocket of her scrubs.

The constant beeping gets my attention. Looking up to notice Rain has her car keys in the air.

"What in the world are you doing?"

"Well, some of us weren't so lucky in the height department. I can't remember where I parked, and I also can't see over the cars to find mine." My head leans back as laughter escapes.

It hits me that my last memory of laughing is nonexistent, combined with the fact that a rare smile appeared on my face the night I first saw her leaving the bar.

Shaking my head, trying to contain the laughter that threatens to come out again, she lets out a "woo" when we find her car. Thankfully, the struggle to get into the car was not as bad as it was in my head. This car is tiny, but I mean, it makes sense.

She hops in and backs out, making her way home. I guess it'll be my home, too, for the next few weeks. Watching the trees go by, the car fills with tension. Looking over, her brows are drawn together, looking as if she's deep in thought.

"What's on your mind?"

"You know we haven't had an actual conversation. I know nothing about you, which is probably insane since you'll be staying with me for a while."

"Well, what do you want to know?"

"Whatever you're willing to share."

"My name is Ghost, I'm 28, and I have a little ball of joy named Snowball."

She can't help but giggle. "Snowball? I love it!"

Of course she does.

"Is that all I get for right now?"

"No, but I want to know about you. You may be the one to be a killer or even worse-creepy."

30

She laughs, "I guess you'll have to sleep with one eye open until you figure that out." She pauses, "My name's Rain, I'm 26, and unfortunately, I don't have a Snowball or any other furry babies."

"Why not?"

Shifting to a frown, "With my shifts at the hospital, I don't have anyone to stay with one while I'm gone."

"Since we're going to be roomies for the foreseeable future, you could always meet Snowball. I'm sure she would enjoy every ounce of extra attention."

What the fuck? For one, I've never been interested in knowing details about anyone, let alone wanting them to meet my dog.

"I'd love that."

"I actually need to call my sister to see if she can watch her for a bit."

She turns the music down as the phone rings. On the third ring, Lily picks up, sounding out of breath, "Do I even want to know what you're doing?"

She huffs, "Well, if you must know, I've been chasing around my crotch goblin since my loving husband decided ice cream was a good idea."

I look over to see Rain stifling a laugh.

Chuckling, "Ice cream does sound like a good idea. Hey, I have some stuff going on. Would you mind watching Snowball for a few days?"

"Of course, I would. Unlike this one, your baby is fluffy. I'll swing by in a bit and pick her up."

31

"You're the best. Thank you, her food is in the pantry, and the key is under the flowerpot. Oh, I need to reschedule dinner, too."

"Got it. That's fine. Just let me know a time that works for you," she huffs again as laughter comes from the background. "I'll talk to you later. Love you."

"Love you too, Lil." Hanging up, I look over to Rain, who's trying not to smile.

"What is it?" not entirely sure what she finds so comical.

A giggle escapes, "Crotch goblin? Your sister sounds amazing."

Smiling to myself, "She is, you'll have to meet her sometime."

"I'd love that."

We return to a comfortable silence as we pull up to her house. It's a simple one-story brick house with a large window in the front. Flowers line the walkway. It looks like her—happy.

Thankfully, they gave me a set of crutches when we left, or it would've been a much bigger struggle attempting to get inside. She carries my bag over one shoulder with her work bag on the other. The most delicious vanilla scent greets me as soon as she opens the door. It's the same smell from earlier. This is going to be a lot harder than I initially thought. The entryway is a light gray color with a table on the left. My attention peaks, noticing she has one picture of who, I would assume, is her mother but no pictures of herself.

I wonder what that's about.

Chapter Six
Rain

He's here. In my bubble. My bubble of safety. What if I'm wrong again?

This is the first time anyone other than Cassi has been in here. Looking back to see him studying the picture of my mother, we have the same eyes.

I hope he doesn't ask.

Motioning toward the living room, he quickly looks up.

Placing his bag by the couch, "I don't have an extra room, but I'll take the couch. Mine's the first door on the right."

He looks at me like I've grown a second head.

"What?"

"There is absolutely no way you're sleeping on a couch. I know you stayed with me at the hospital last night. You need to get a good night's sleep."

Before I can argue, he looks at me, daring me to say another word.

"Fine. I'll bring out an extra pillow and some blankets. The bathroom is the door on the left. I'm going to shower, and then we can order something to eat."

His gaze softens, "Thank you."

Making my way to the shower, exhaustion hits, making the sound of a good night's sleep sound even more appealing. Stripping down, the clothes sadly miss the basket once again. The steam fills the bathroom from the scalding water. Most of the knots are here to stay despite rolling my neck side to side. Finally able to rid my body of a small amount of tension, the pale pink bath rug tickles my feet as the oversized towel removes the droplets from my skin. The water drips from the ends of my hair as the comb detangles the overwhelming amount of knots. A shirt from my half-empty closet slips over my head, followed by cotton shorts that slide up my legs. With one last look in the mirror, my opponent awaits- the hallway closet.

I should really rethink putting the blankets on the top shelf.

Standing there with my hands on my hips, daggers shoot out of my eyes. Hopping, I'm barely able to knock them off, almost failing to catch them before they land directly on my face. Closing the closet door, the living room comes into view.

Chapter Seven

Ghost

My eyes almost bulge out of my head when she comes into the room. Hair wet, those legs on display. She's the most beautiful thing I've ever seen.

My decision is set in stone.

I want her. Everything. Every detail.

I was trying to stay away, 1 really was, but at this moment, failure is very likely.

She makes her way over, her hips swaying with every step.

"Here you go. If you need an extra one, just let me know. Did you think about what you want for dinner?"

"Thank you. How does a pizza sound? Here's my debit card. Go ahead and get whatever you want."

"That sounds great, but I'm not using your money. I've got it."

Pinning her with a stare, she moves her weight from one foot to the other.

"Fine, but I'm paying next time."

That's my good girl. Get a grip. She's just being nice. Focus.

As she walks into the kitchen, which is connected to the living room, my gaze automatically lowers. She's going to be the death of me, and she's completely unaware of it just like the night at the bar.

"What do you want to drink?" as her head pops around the corner.

"It doesn't matter. Whatever you have is good with me."

A few minutes later, she walks back in with two drinks and her phone between her head and shoulder. She reaches it to me, our fingers barely brushing. Looking up, I meet her eyes, but she quickly turns away. She curls up on the opposite side of the couch while she reaches for the remote on the coffee table careful to keep her distance.

She surprises me when she asks, "I have a question, which is very serious, what kind of movies do you like?"

Studying her face, "I typically watch action or comedy. A mix of both is probably my favorite, though. I'll even take one for the team and watch one of those sappy movies if you want."

She giggles. "They're not sappy. Okay, well, a lot of them are, but in my defense, there are a lot of great ones. They'll turn your heart into a puddle."

"You're awfully convincing. Pick your favorite, and I'll be the judge," raising an eyebrow at her. "My heart better be in a puddle by the time this is over, or it's an automatic failure."

"Yay! Deal."

She's beaming.

Yep, I think I'll be a fan of these "romance" movies she loves so much. I am a complete goner for the pint-sized woman beside me.

She scrutinizes each movie, trying to pick the perfect one, but immediately runs to the door when a couple of knocks get her attention. Coming back in, holding two pizzas, she's grinning from ear to ear.

She sets them on the coffee table and returns to her mission of finding the perfect movie. She finally settles on *The Notebook*.

Oh lord.

Leaning forward, grabbing us each a slice of pizza, the aroma surrounds us. She takes it without looking, already submerged within the first two seconds of the movie. We finish an entire pizza an hour in. Looking over, her eyes are still locked on the screen. The lamp enhances her profile- the perfect nose, soft pink lips, and hair that looks like silk. My eyes return to the TV before she catches me staring.

The end credits start rolling. She's wearing a smile that lights up her entire face, with her eyes twinkling by the light glow of the lamp.

"See what I mean?" almost bouncing up and down, "absolute perfection. What did you think?"

Admittedly, she was right. It was pretty good.

Dramatically rolling my eyes, unable to hold back a grin of my own, "I guess it wasn't too terrible."

"I told you!"

"Go ahead and pick another one. Let's see if they're all tolerable."

She grabs the remote, scrolling through more options, and finally lands on another. As it starts, her eyes begin to grow heavy. She's slowly giving in to exhaustion. Sleep ends up taking over. To my surprise, my attention stays on the TV until something moves on my good leg. Looking down to see her small feet- toenails painted pink, she has managed to scoot down and is now taking up most of the couch. Grabbing a thick blanket from the back of the sofa, I throw it over us. Not wanting to risk waking her, I scoot down just enough so my head can lean back on the couch. It's my turn for sleep to embrace me.

Chapter Eight
Rain

Waking up to sunlight directly in my eyes, paired with the sound of soft snoring, something heavy is lying on my legs. Reluctantly opening my eyes to see Ghost, in what must be an extremely uncomfortable position, with an arm resting on my legs.

Oh.

Sitting up and slipping out of his hold fails when his grip on my legs tightens. Trying to move his arm again without waking him up is successful as my legs slide over the edge of the couch. Going down the hallway, the cold floor freezes my feet. I jump as my reflection stares back at me. Mascara from yesterday circles my eyes. Every strand of hair on my head is in a different direction. Almost slinging the drawer from the vanity, my hand lands on a brush, which feels as though it will break as it attempts to run through my hair. Face wash manages to to make me look semi-presentable so I don't scare the poor man.

Walking back into the living room, the morning sunlight makes his face glow. As his eyes slowly open, his gaze finds mine. I quickly turn away, unable to get into the kitchen fast enough. Rummaging through the refrigerator, only to realize that there is absolutely nothing for us to eat. My breath catches as my head turns to find Ghost looking over my shoulder. *Nobody get's this close to me. My childhood taught me that lesson. How did he even come in here without making a sound?*

Turning to look up at him, I take in his towering frame.

He looks from me to the refrigerator, chuckling, "That looks a lot like mine."

"What, empty?"

"Yep. What do you want to eat? I can go grab something for us."

I look at him with a brow raised. Confusion covers his face, eventually morphing into understanding as he looks down.

"Shit, I mean, I can still go. I know you must be hungry."

Just as he says that my stomach lets out a loud growl. I guess I am even after that pizza last night.

"You are absolutely not driving, but if you insist, you can come with me."

"I'll settle for that."

We end up in the mile-long line at the drive-thru. Quickly realizing my fingers have been tapping on the steering wheel, they stop.

We pull up and order. Of course, he insists on paying again. Pulling into a parking spot overlooking the busy road, he hands me my food and starts devouring his. My shoulders drop ever so slightly as his attention isn't directly on me anymore. The curiosity get the best of me as thoughts swirl through my mind.

Glancing over at him, "Tell me something."

His head tilts back on the headrest. "Let's see. I moved here four years ago. I wasn't planning on staying, but I ended up falling in love with the city and never left. What about you?"

"I was born and raised here. I grew up a few blocks from the house. I guess I never really made it far. I've thought about leaving but could never bring myself to do it."

With blades of grass between my fingers, I inhale a deep breath. I hear the neighbors laugh and bicycles flying past as my eyes open to see fluffy clouds slowly moving by. "Rain, come in! You've been out there all day. You need to eat." A small smile crosses my face. My mother's always been a ray of sunshine. Always putting others first. I head into the house, where a peanut butter sandwich is waiting. "Thank you, mom." I watch as she walks over to the table. "You're welcome, sweetie. Now, eat up." As I put my dishes away, I can't help but crave the fresh air again. My feet carry me back to the yard, grass between my toes, and continue to watch the clouds go by. Always. I promise myself I'll always be free.

"Hey, are you ok? You kind of zoned out."

"Oh yeah, I'm good. I just remembered that growing up, I would always lie in the grass watching the clouds," the words pour out before I can stop them.

He faces forward, looking up at the sky where big fluffy clouds move slowly, unlike the chaos beneath them.

"I never really paid attention to them until you mentioned it," his face morphs into wonder.

Ringing interrupts our peace, snapping him out of his trance.

"Yeah?" irritation evident in his voice. I think he may have been enjoying this as much as I have. "I'll look into it."

The change instantly makes my guard go back up.

Chapter Nine

Ghost

Really? This is the moment River decided to call. Once again, interrupting the peace I've started to enjoy.

"Is everything okay?" a look of concern on her face.

"Yeah, do you mind if we head back? I have a work thing I need to deal with."

Her face drops for an instant but goes back to her happy self. I'm beginning to wonder if her face tells what she's genuinely feeling or if she wears a mask like I do most of the time.

The backpack nearly slips from my shoulder as the swarm of people pushes each other through the hallway. My head jerks back as my bag is pulled backward causing me to stumble. The other kids stare, but keep moving. I'm circled by four guys that are twice my size. With the locker pressed against my back, I'm out of options.

"You smell that boys? What is that? Smells like stale cigarettes and straight trash." They all join in laughing as my fist clenches at my side. My face never changes. I've spent the past few years training myself to never show emotion. That's a lesson I learned from these guys as well as dear ole dad. Their faces fall as they realise I'm not going to burst into tears like their other victims. With one last shove, they continue on down the hallway. Keeping my head down, my feet carry me to class. Diving into the seat in the back corner, my body curls in trying to make myself invisible. If only I was a ghost.

The fresh air flowing through the car brings me back to the present. Music plays softly in the background. Once we pull into her driveway, I pull my crutches out of the back seat and follow her up the walkway. Glancing over at the picture of her mother again, my curiosity peaks.

I'm going to have to ask her about that.

Taking my spot on the couch, my phone slides out of my pocket. Dialing Ace, he grumbles about the call with River. Someone has reportedly seen our guy entering what we thought was an abandoned house.

As far as they could tell, he was empty-handed.

Then what the hell was he doing?

That house is now obviously the primary focus of our surveillance, which Luke and Cam primarily cover.

Hanging up the phone, my ears perk up, listening for Rain's footsteps. Failing to hear anything, worry begins to take over. Beginning my way down the hallway, she said the one on the right, right? Knocking, my ears strain to listen.

Nothing.

The worry consumes me at this point.

Barging in, she's sitting on the edge of her bed, rocking back and forth with her hands covering her face. Instantly rushing over, ignoring the fire in my leg, my knees hit the floor in front of her. My hands circle her wrists, carefully moving them down to her lap. Her eyes are squeezed shut. Quick, shallow breaths leave her mouth.

"Little bird, I need you to open your eyes and look at me."

Reluctantly, she opens them. Tears run down her face.

"Breathe with me. In and out."

Slowly, her breathing returns to normal, and her tears come to a stop.

"I'm sorry. I didn't want you to see me like this."

"I'll gladly be the one to ground you. What's going on in that mind of yours?"

"Today, when we were talking, I remembered when I was younger. My mother fussed at me about coming inside to eat. I had spent the entire day watching the clouds go by," she said, taking a deep breath and avoiding my eyes. I put one finger under her chin and lift her face until she looks at me.

"Does this have to do with the picture downstairs?"

"Yes. That same day, she was doing everything possible to stay busy. She looked exhausted—bloodshot eyes with dark circles underneath. I don't think she realized I saw that side of her. I had seen it several times before, but that day was different. She sounded the same, but something was just off," she closes her eyes and she begins again, "You see, my dad had always been very involved. He was everything someone could ask for in a father. But the older I got, the more I realized he would go to work early and wouldn't come home for days. Never a hair out of place, though. That's when I noticed her taking on more. Over the years, I couldn't help but watch the weight of the world slowly come down on her shoulders. A few days before that, he hadn't come home. Every day, I asked when he would be back. All she could say was, "Soon, honey." and she would, once again, busy herself— the day after is when my world stopped. I had peeked into her room after searching the entire house, to find her curled up on the bed sobbing. She shut down that day. Since then, I was always afraid of what I would find when I got home. I spent the next few years taking care of her. Until one day, I came home, and she just wasn't there."

Wrapping my arms around her as her head presses against my chest, "I promise you're safe. I've got you. No child should ever have to experience something like that. I'm so sorry today triggered that-"

She cuts me off, craning her neck to meet my eyes, "No, today was the best day I've had in a very long time. It made me feel like that day when I was happy. Not a care in the world. Thank you."

My lips press against her forehead, and I whisper, "You'll always be safe with me. I promise."

She takes a deep breath- her entire body relaxes.

"Stay right here."

Walking across the hall, the warm water soaks the washcloth. Placing one hand under her chin, the warmth runs over her face.

"Why did she never leave?" unable to keep the curiosity at bay.

"She wanted the fairy tale ending. She was obsessed with being the perfect wife. She dealt with everything no matter how much it broke her."

The thoughts of my mother refusing to leave my father overtake my mind causing a wave of nausea to take hold of me. Abruptly standing, I scoop her into my arms, one arm against her back and one under her legs,

"Wait! You're leg. You're not supposed to even be putting all your weight on it, much less carrying me," she panics.

Pressing her closer, "Please let me be the one to take care of you this time."

She sighs, surprisingly not fighting me on this. The pain grips me, but my body somehow manages to relax as peace overtakes her.

Chapter Ten

Rain

Every ounce of tension dissipates from my body. His warmth, his arms wrapped around me, the feeling when he brings me a little closer with every step. The doubt that was initially in my mind still lingers. My instincts of someone being a protector has been wrong in the past, but now I'm not so sure

"Here, lay down here for a little bit. I'll be right back." He lays me down gently on the couch.

Grabbing a blanket, he covers me as if one breeze on my skin will turn me into an ice cube. I can't help but smile to myself. He turns the TV on, searching for a romance movie. My heart melts.

After finding one he thinks I'll enjoy, he turns toward the kitchen. A second later, I hear pots and pans clink together and cabinets open and close.

I desperately need to get groceries.

A few minutes later, he comes out holding a peanut butter sandwich on a small plate in one hand and a drink in the other with a small smile. Sitting up, the blanket he so carefully tucked in falls to my lap. He reaches me the plate. Studying my hands, tears threaten to escape.

It's just like mom used to make.

"Thank you," I whisper, looking up at him.

He sits down, causing the couch to sink in. He leaves enough room between us to make me feel comfortable. There goes another brick from the wall I've made for myself.

Shaking my head, taking one small bite at a time, I inhale the entire sandwich.

Wiping my mouth, I whisper, "My mom was supposed to be there for me, and she wasn't. All those feelings just came back in full force. I'm sorry you had to see that," unable to meet his intense stare.

Tilting my face, forcing my eyes to meet his, "Don't you dare apologize. The same thing happened with my mom. Some people just check out sometimes, and it's a very, very difficult thing to accept, especially when it's someone who's meant to protect you."

We sit in comfortable silence until a part of the movie makes him let out a chuckle.

My eyes grow heavy. Maybe a quick nap won't hurt.

Waking up an hour later, my head rises as the realization hits that I was lying on his chest. Unable to fully raise up, I look around, my eyes settle on the large arm wrapped around my shoulders. My body jerks away.

I can't let myself get close to him.

Making my way to my bedroom, the door closes carefully behind me. Digging through the drawer, I finally find the pink, fluffy socks I was looking for. Each sock slips on, causing me to sigh as the warmth engulfs my feet. My head leans back as the ceiling begins looking like the most interesting thing in the world.

Deep breath in. Deep breath out.

Standing to return to the living room, an old paintbrush on the dresser catches my eye. My breath catches. I haven't touched a brush since before Mom went downhill. I'm not sure why it's even lying there. Glancing back at my closet, my feet carry me forward with hesitation. Large cardboard boxes fill the bottom, only leaving enough room for my shoes. Grabbing the first one and removing the tape, my hands shuffle through the contents inside. Nothing. Moving to the one sitting below it, my eyes land on what I'm searching for. A clean blank canvas brushes my hand.

Maybe I shouldn't. I'm not even sure what I would paint.

The memory from earlier flashes through my mind. The peace she took from me. The childhood she stole. The rage that ran through me returns as I recall the helplessness I felt today.

Bottles of paint sit at the bottom of the box next to a smaller cardboard box containing old paintbrushes matching the one on the dresser. Splatters of paint that were never washed off still cover the handles. My hands grip the extra blanket on my bed. It spreads out in the corner of the room, facing the window. Taking in the clouds in the sky, the bird hopping around its nest on the tree branch that knocks against my window during storms, and the children laughing as they cross the road, emotions overwhelm me. Unscrewing the top of each bottle, a drop of paint lands on the tray. The brush dips in, the soft bristles of the brush meet the canvas. Color after color, layers, dimension, and depth hide the plain white material. My heart is on laying out for everyone to see.

This isn't enough.

Walking back to the closet, my eyes search for more. Thankfully, one last canvas remains, begging to be used. Carefully setting the first one to the side, I begin again. The delicate brush glides against it, but as it does, something runs down my face. These feelings have been bottled up for so long, they're all finally coming out at once. Tears blur my vision. I continue until the paintbrush falls onto the blanket.

My shoulders sag as I let the tears flow.

Deep breaths. Everything's okay.

A sense of relief washes over me as my eyes take in what's in front of me. Again, the art expresses something I've never been able to put into words. Picking up each paintbrush, I realize the paint is caked on my arms.

My thoughts wander on the way to the bathroom. The water runs blue as the paint swirls around the drain. Rinsing until the water clears, my reflection looks back at me in the mirror. Puffy eyes stare back at me. After scrubbing them clean, my arms are raw. The brushes lie on the counter to dry.

Opening the door, lost in thought, my front hits something that feels eerily similar to a brick wall. Nearly falling back, large hands grab my waist, looking up to find ice-blue eyes staring down at me.

"You alright?" A look of concern covers his face. His hair is disheveled.

"Yes, I was in my own little world. I'm sorry."

"Don't apologize. I was in the way."

Feeling heat moving up my neck, knowing my face will look like a tomato in about two seconds, I duck my head and squeeze past him.

A hand grips my arm, "Hey, are you sure everything's okay? It looks like you've been crying."

"Oh yeah, I'm completely fine," I say, pulling my arm away and scurrying back to my room.

As I close the door, my eyes land on the face in front of me, which is currently looking behind me at the result of my slight mental breakdown. My door closes as my hands meet my face.

My head shakes as I dig around in my closet for what seems like forever, deciding on cut-off shorts and a t-shirt, my hair goes up into a ponytail, and my sandals, which were halfway under the bed, slip onto my feet. The living room is empty. Peeking around the corner, he's sitting at the kitchen table with his brows drawn, staring at his phone. He doesn't notice my lingering.

53

SHADOWS AND DECEPTION

Chapter Eleven

Ghost

Should I count to ten or take deep breaths?
I know whichever I choose still won't help lower my blood pressure.

Staring at my phone, my vision tints red. Multiple girls at the local hospital have shared stories that align with the drugging incidents we've been tracking. "Tyler" hasn't so much as uttered a peep despite his condition—loyal to the wrong side. According to Ace, the boy hasn't broken. Between Luke and Cam taking a deep dive into his phone and background, they're certain something will pop up.

The hair on the back of my neck raises at the sense of being watched. My head snaps up to see Rain standing in the doorway for who knows how long.

"Are you okay?" her eyebrows furrowed together.

"Yeah, it's just Ace."

"I'm being nosey, I'm sorry," looking down.

"Hey, even though we don't know each other very well, I'll tell you whatever you want to know," staring into her eyes, making sure she knows how serious I am. Raising one eyebrow, holding my pinky up, "Pinky promise."

The corners of her mouth tilt up as she brings her finger up to meet mine, "Same with me. I was going to get groceries, so we don't wither away. Do you want anything specific?"

"I'll eat anything. Here, I'll pay," I say, reaching into my wallet, taking out my debit card, and reaching it out to her.

She makes no move to take it, "Listen, thank you, but we'll take turns because there is no way you are paying for everything while you're here. Text me if you want me to pick up anything." Shrugging her bag higher on her shoulder, she turns to leave.

"Thank you," I whisper.

Hearing the door close, my eyes close as my head leans back. Opening them to stare at the ceiling.

This was easier on my own.

Two minutes later, the door opens again. Already on high alert, I jump up, not expecting Rain to be standing there. She startles when she sees me.

"Are you okay?" taking a step closer.

"Yes, oh, this is embarrassing. Never mind," she turns to walk out again.

"Wait. What's embarrassing?"

"Well, I was going to see if you wanted to come shopping with me."

The anger from a few minutes ago seems to lessen, "Of course, I would. Let's go," walking past her and out the door.

Her eyes widen as if she can't believe the answer was yes to something so simple. Waiting by the passenger door, she walks down the walkway, still looking lost in thought. Once she notices that I'm waiting to open her door, her face lights up. She slides in. Rounding the front of the door, I plop down, or at least attempt to anyway. The steering wheel digs into my chest, and my knees are crammed on either side, "What the fuck?" I whisper.

She leans back, laughing, gripping her stomach. Between gasps, she manages to say, "I didn't know you would be driving earlier, or I would've moved the seat back."

Pinning her with a look that only makes her laugh harder, backing the seat up only helps a small amount.

Starting the car, "Are you trying to be part of the windshield or something? Why is the seat so far up?"

She wiggles her legs in front of her, "See these? They are the complete opposite of those," pointing at my legs unable to contain my own laughter that escapes.

The relatively short drive consists of drumming my fingers on the steering wheel as Rain throws her head back and forth like she's in a rock band. Pulling into the parking spot, looking over to see her with a wide grin.

"You ready?"

"Duh! Let's go shop," she hops out. Just as my door opens, she pulls on my hand to get out. The cracking and popping of my knees is audible as I stand.

We walk up and down every aisle, squeezing through the occasional sea of people. She grabs what feels like everything and throws it into the cart, not waiting for my response when she asks my opinion. It's inevitable to watch her in wonder.

This is my favorite side of her—the one where she's in her own little world, just simply living.

Once we get to the checkout, she huffs in defeat as she sees my card being shoved to the cashier before she can beat me to it.

As we walk into the parking lot, all I hear is, "Watch this!" She runs and jumps on the end of the cart and hangs on for dear life. Her hair blows in the wind as her laughter fills the air. Surprisingly, I decide to join when hopping up on my side. We nearly miss hitting a car on the way down the middle. Once we get to her car, we both get down still laughing. We load the bags in the back seat and begin our way back to the house.

Before putting the car in park, Rain hops out of the car. I look over to see her attempting to grab every bag. Walking over, my arm snakes around her, taking them all out of her hands.

She lets out a squeal, barely able to squeak, "How on earth did you do that? I didn't even hear you come up."

"It's a specialty; now let me get these."

Reluctantly, she lets go but jogs up the walkway to open the door. Walking into the kitchen, every bag drops on the counter.

Did she buy everything in the store?

After putting half of the things in the wrong place, we settle on a system that consists of me reaching her things as she puts it away. Turning around, she's beaming as she holds two pints of ice cream and an unopened popcorn box.

A chuckle creeps out, "And what's that for?"

"Well," she draws out, "I was thinking we could watch another movie tonight." Suddenly bashful, "But if you don't want to or have other plans, I completely get- "

Before she can finish that sentence, the box of popcorn is out of her hand. Every cabinet opens and closes in an attempt to find a bowl. After finally finding one that will work, I turn back to her, "Go pick us something out. I'll be in there in a minute." She turns to skip out into the living room. The tension she carried yesterday seems to have lessened- at least a little bit.

Rain's already sitting on the couch, biting her lip engrossed in whatever she's watching. Smiling to myself, I sit next to her with the bowl of popcorn. She glances at me before she quickly looks away as bright red coats her neck rising to her face.

Clearing my throat, "What are you watching?"

"Oh, I just clicked on something. Do you want to watch something else?"

"No, this is perfect." I say as she reaches for the bowl. Returning to the kitchen to grab our drinks, they threaten to spill over the rim.

Sitting down, she scoots over, holding the bowl out, looking at me expectantly. A grin appears as popcorn fills my hand. Sitting back, we turn our attention to the screen. As the blanket covers her, the feeling of her eyes on me never leaves causing the corner of my mouth to turn up. She whips her head back to the screen. Glancing over to study her face- those lips, big brown eyes with long eyelashes, a glow covering her skin that I haven't noticed before.

Stop.

She lets out a yawn, her eyes suddenly becoming heavy. As her eyes close, she slowly starts leaning closer and closer until her head is on my shoulder. My entire body tenses.

I'm not good for her. I'm nothing short of a monster.

As the movie ends, her eyes are still closed, and even breaths leave her lips. I shift to the edge of the couch and slide my hand behind her back and under her legs. My steps stay light, attempting not to wake her. Her bedroom door carefully opens—padding across the carpet to gently place her on her bed. Unable to refrain from leaning down and kissing her forehead, inhaling the scent of her hair. Closing her door, my phone begins ringing from down the hall.

Where the hell is it?

Shoving my hands between the cushions, my hand grips the cause of the noise as it silences. My eyebrows draw together-it's Ace. He never calls this late. My stomach turns, dread seeps into my bones. "Hey, man. What's up?"

"Dude, I've been trying to call you forever." He breathes heavily, "hang on." The call ends. Panic begins to rise. Raising my thumb to redial his number, banging on the front door makes me jump. The door swings open, revealing a red-faced Ace holding his fist up to bang on the door again.

"Will you stop? I just laid Rain down in her bed. She's exhausted. Get in here." Annoyance paired with relief runs through me, "What the hell has you all worked up?"

"The piece of shit that shot you," he breathes out, "still hasn't said anything, but we saw someone come out of the house."

"Did you get them?"

"No, we couldn't unless we wanted to give up our position."

A hand runs through my hair.

This can never be easy, can it?

Realizing that I've been pacing a hole in the floor, I drop down on the couch, throwing my head back and closing my eyes. The couch sinks as Ace sits down.

"There is a slight amount of good news."

Turning my head, "That would be great right about now. What is it?"

"The number of women being taken from the bar has significantly lowered since we got those two off the streets."

It doesn't need to just lower. It needs to end.

"That's a start, but we aren't stopping until the one behind this is dead."

"I agree 100%."

"Do you want to crash here tonight? We can look into it in the morning after we attempt to get some rest." His bouncing leg slows, "Yeah, I think that's a good idea. Thanks."

Blindly reaching for the remote on the coffee table, we begin going through the channels when I do the unthinkable. The sappiest looking movie pops up on the screen- voluntarily.

What is this woman doing to me?

"What the hell are you watching?" he chuckles.

"Shut up and just watch it."

Unable to hold in the laughter at the sight of Ace fully immersed in the TV, "I told you!"

"Would you stop? He's going to kiss her!" His eyes stay glued to the screen. A few seconds later, he jumps up, "It's about time he did it! Hey, you know it wouldn't be the worst thing if we watched another one."

My eyebrows raise as a smirk forms, "I never thought I'd see the day."

Rolling his eyes, he sits back against the couch, folding his arms over his chest. The opening scene fades as my eyes close, and I drift into darkness.

A cool breeze grazes across my skin as my eyes crack open. Still groggy, my head turns while taking in my surroundings. My favorite vanilla scent is paired with every window in this house now open.

Making my way towards the humming coming from the kitchen, I stop in my tracks at the sight of Rain wiping down the counters in an oversized shirt and shorts, her hair thrown up, and not a stitch of makeup on. Leaning against the doorway, I appreciate the sight before me.

She's beautiful.

Her lips barely move as she sings a song only she knows. Noticing the dishes in the sink, in a few steps she's beside me, causing her to let out a tiny scream.

"Can you please start making at least a little bit of noise?" her hand grasps at her chest.

Chuckling, "I'll try." The faucet squeaks as it turns on. The soap bottle makes tiny bubbles float in front of my face as a faint giggle comes from behind me.

Smirking, "Is something funny, little bird?"

"Nope." A giggle still slips free.

The sound of chaos travels in as Luke and Cam barge through the front door.

Cam bounces through the house with an overwhelming amount of energy for this time of morning. His eyes land on Rain as he walks into the kitchen, which causes his face to light up.

Walking over, he throws an arm around her, "How's my favorite half-pint?"

Before he can answer, he meets my eyes and immediately raises his hands in surrender. "Sorry, man." A chuckle leaves him as he walks back into the living room.

With a glance back while following him out of the kitchen, Rain's smiling while she's shaking her head.

My eyes widen, "What the hell is everyone doing here?"

Luke is the only one who acknowledges anything even came out of my mouth. "We're just picking up Ace. We have some stuff to go over."

Looking over to see Ace sitting in the same spot that he was in last night, rubbing a hand over his face. Cassi apparently got the invitation to show up, too. She stands in front of him with both hands on her hips, complaining about something she heard on the way over.

Luke continues chewing on his toothpick, "Alright, everyone out. We have shit to do today, so you can complain later," throwing Cassi a glance.

She rolls her eyes, "Ugh. I'll see you later, Rain!"

She opens and slams the front door before Rain can respond. Ace stands as he stretches his arms above his head. We all stare, expecting an explanation.

"Nope, It's way too early. Let's get this over with," walking over to the door.

"We'll let you know if we find out anything." Cam pipes up as they all walk out of the front door.

CJ MCKINNEY

Well, that was a lot.

SHADOWS AND DECEPTION

Chapter Twelve

Rain

My humming continues as everything calms in the other room,

"Go get dressed. We're leaving in 20."

Ghost pops his head into the kitchen and looks at me like I've grown a second head. "Wait, why?"

"It's a surprise," batting my eyelashes.

"Fine," grumbling as he walks up the stairs.

Someone's not a morning person.

He walks back into the kitchen, catching my stare, and the corners of his mouth turn up. "You coming?"

"Yep. Let's go." After throwing the broom into the closet and slipping my sandals on, my eyes take in the morning sunlight beaming over everything, making it glow from the porch. He bolts past as he opens the car door for me. Nodding a thank you, realizing he hasn't used the crutches past day two while he's been here.

At least he tried.

"Are you going to tell me where we're going?"

"Nope. You'll see when we get there. You'll love it, though."

"This sounds fun," his eyes light up.

He has no idea.

We pull up in front of a doctor's office. *His* doctor's office, might I add. Glancing over, the realization sinks in.

"No, absolutely not. I do not want to be poked at, especially this early in the morning."

"Come on, you baby. Get out," as he pins me with a stare, crossing his arms in a pout.

"Fine, I guess I'll just go in myself."

Two can play at this game.

"Like hell you are. I can't believe you got me here. I'll admit that was good."

Explaining to the receptionist that we're here for a follow-up appointment, she smiles softly and turns back to type a mile a minute on her computer. Looking back, I see Ghost taking everything in with a scowl.

Turning back to the receptionist, she says, "You're all checked in, sweetie. Just have a seat in the waiting room."

Grabbing his hand, we march over to the germ pit—oh, I meant the "waiting room." His fingers tap on the plastic seat as his good leg bounces.

"Would you stop that? You're making me nervous."

He immediately stops. "I'm sorry. I really dislike offices if you haven't noticed."

"This will be quick. Then we can go back home-"

An older lady with short gray hair cuts us short. "You both can come back now." Her eyes crease at the side as she smiles.

The smell of disinfectant almost knocks us over. The white walls are all but missing padding and a strait jacket.

Okay, I can see why he doesn't like offices now.

He's thankfully following close behind as we enter an exam room. He hops up on the table and subconsciously begins swinging his legs like a child.

"He'll be in here in just a moment."

"You know I'm perfectly fine, right? No need to be here." He makes a move to get down.

"Don't even think about it. This is the only one you need to come to if you're absolutely refusing to continue following up with him-"

We're cut off again by the same man from the hospital. He looks Ghost over from head to toe as his face morphs into disapproval. With a sigh, he accepts that few to none of his directions were followed after discharge.

Oops.

He pushes his glasses to the bridge of his nose, "How's everything been?"

Ghost starts without hesitation, "I'm all healed up, Doc. I haven't had any issues since the last time I saw you. Can we go now?"

"Hold on just a second. Now, tell me how things have really been in the few days you've been recuperating."

He swallows, looking like a child who's just been caught, "I really am feeling better. I have some pain when I put weight on it, but it's bearable."

"I can work with that. You only have a couple of stitches that need to be removed in a few days."

He turns to face me, "I've seen you in the ER before, right?"

Nodding my head, "Yes, sir."

"I'll give you this set to remove his sutures. If you have any questions or are uncomfortable, call the office, and they'll schedule an appointment for him to come back." Glancing over, Ghost stares at the doctor, his eyebrows meeting his hairline.

The man looks back at Ghost disapprovingly. "Just be careful walking on it. Let me know if you have any issues." He walks out, shaking his head, and closes the door.

Ghost's head snaps toward mine, "You can really take these out?"

"Yes, it's part of my job. I can do it with my eyes closed at this point," chuckling. He lets out a sigh of relief.

Thanks for the confidence.

He hops off the table, wincing, but shakes it off. He glances back as he grips my hand, dragging me out of the office. As we pass the check-out desk, the woman holds a finger up, attempting to have us stop.

Of course he ignores it.

I mouth, "Sorry."

His grip tightens around my hand until we're standing by the passenger door. Looking up, he stares with a grin, "Come on, little bird, hop in."

"What on earth do you think you're doing? You are not about to drive my car just because of what he said."

He opens the door anyway, scooting me inside, "Oh, but I am." My eyes widen.

Before I can say anything, my door closes as he rounds the front of my car. The one he's about to drive as he's half-injured. He doesn't attempt to hide that he's laughing at my expression. His smile drops as seriousness flows over his face, "Trust me. I promise you I'll always keep you safe." Holding out a pinky, his smirk returns.

"Fine." Matching his expression, I wrap my finger around his.

He straightens as he faces forward and floors it as he peels out of the parking lot. I can't help but release a squeal- 50% terror and 50% excitement. As a wave of adrenaline washes over me, my head leans back while my eyes. My finger traces the door handle until it stops on the button, causing the window to roll down. The breeze instantly weaves through my hair as a smile takes over my face. Turning my head, I can barely make out Ghost sporting the same expression while he holds his hand out the window, moving it up and down with the wind.

He weaves in and out of traffic, skyscrapers tower above us. Realization hits me as I see people sitting at their desks, raking their hands through their hair or lost in thought as they walk along the sidewalk, swaying side to side with the movement of others beside them. We're all just part of an overall story. Each of us lives in our own little worlds tied together with a little bow.

The horn blaring brings me out of a philosophical haze I entered. My entire body jerks as my arms automatically grip the door handle and what I believe is his arm. Glancing over, he's laughing without an ounce of concern.

Yelling over the noise, "You could've killed us!"

"But I didn't. That's what matters, isn't it?" his expression never changes.

He has a point. Maybe.

Returning to the sight before us, I continue to take in everyone around us. He never hits the break until we're pulling into the driveway. My entire body buzzes with adrenaline.

I feel a hand on mine. "I'm sorry if I scared you-"

"Can we do that again?"

"Of course. Anything for you." Letting go of my hand, he comes around to open my door.

"Thank you, kind sir," dramatically dipping my head, waving my hand in the air.

He bursts into laughter. Unable to keep a serious expression any longer, I join him. Once we're able to catch our breath, we look at each other and attempt to not begin another round of laughing.

"Come on," turning as a giggle escapes.

He follows without question.

SHADOWS AND DECEPTION

Chapter Thirteen

Ghost

The nerves begin to take over. Ignoring them, I grab her attention as she walks out of the bathroom.

"I was wondering if you would do something for me?"

She takes me in, "Are you okay? Are you in pain?"

The corners of my mouth turn up, "Yes, I'm fine. Here."

Walking over to the couch, my hand grips the corner pulling it out just enough to reach behind. Sliding out the canvas her mouth drops.

"What? Why? Wait, how did you get that?"

My free hand runs up the back of my neck. "I had Luke bring it over this morning. I saw your paintings, and thought maybe you could paint one of me. I mean, if you want to."

Her mouth drops as her eyes widen. She shakes her head bring her out of her daze. "Yeah, I would love to. Come on."

Scooting the couch back, she leads us to her room. Hair bows cover her dresser, the blankets are still thrown back, but everything else is tidy. The blanket from yesterday is still in the corner. When her eyes met mine, I knew the look of pain far too well. As she closed the door, I tried to take everything in as quickly as possible despite my better judgement.

"Here." She reaches her hand out while studying the canvas in my hand. A look of reluctance and nervousness cover her face as she takes it.

"You don't have to if you don't want to. I just thought it may be something that you enjoy," the bed squeaks as my weight lands on the edge.

"I do enjoy it. I did anyway at one point." She hesitates while her focus lands on the two paintings still leaning against the wall. "It's been awhile, and those were the first I've done in years."

"They're amazing. You know you have a gift for it."

She scoffs, "I wouldn't go that far."

Her knees meet the soft blanket as she squeezes paint out of each bottle. Her brows draw as she looks around. Remembering her paint brushes were on the counter this morning, I bolt into the bathroom swiping them all in one hand. She looks up as I step back into the room holding them out to her. Her face relaxes as she sees what's in my hand.

"Thank you. I completely forgot they were in there," a soft smile covers her face.

Taking my place once again on the bed, her focus returns to me as she takes in all of my features. Her delicate hands wrap around the handle of a brush as the paint glides across the blank space. She's seemingly entered her own world. Selfishly, it gives me a chance to take her in. Tension doesn't have her in its grasp and her worries are forgotten at this moment in time.

Her lips part as her eyes bounce between me and the brush.

She hesitates, "Since you know a little bit about my parents, you can tell me about yours if you want."

Grimacing as another fist connects to my cheek. I swear his eyes have turned black. As long as his attention is on me and away from my mother and Lily, everything will be okay. My fist swings, barely clipping his jaw, only to infuriate him further.

A frown appears at the memory. "My father wasn't the best to say the least. Long story short, he's no longer around. My mom took off with my sister so she's not in the picture. I thankfully reconnected with Lily, which you heard when we left the hospital." The thought of my little sister eases the memory.

"I'm so sorry. I didn't know." Realizing her brush strokes have stopped, she continues.

"It's alright. I met the guys through that nightmare. We're family so it was worth it."

A soft smile appears, "It's the same way with Cass. We met when we were kids. She was the only one that saw that I was struggling. She would keep the attention off of me so I could sleep in class. It was the only time I could between jobs and taking care of mom."

"Why did you have to work so much?"

"If I didn't we would've lost everything. She was barely even living so I had to scrape up every penny to support both of us."

Heat takes over my body at the thought of her not having help- of her being alone like I was for so long. My eyes close while deep breaths enter my lungs. Looking up, she's taking me in. It's as though she's seeing me in a way that nobody ever has.

For the first time in my life, I don't want to be a ghost.

My thumb rubs circles on the wool blanket as an attempt at distracting myself from the uncomfortable thought. The silence envelopes us she closes down again assuming she's shared enough of herself today, but I'll take whatever she's willing to give.

Ignoring the cramping that has overtaken, my attention has been on her this entire time making the pain bearable.

She blows a piece of hair out of her face, "I'm finished."

My mouth opens, but words refuse to come out as she turns the canvas around. She managed to get every single detail down to my pores. She may have even included details I was oblivious to.

She giggles at my response, "Do you like it?" She bites her lip as those eyes that light me on fire meet mine.

"It's amazing, Rain. I'm speechless. Don't stop painting. Please."

"Thank you," she whispers, "I forgot what it was like. I forgot how much I love painting."

Without thinking, my thumb reaches up to brush against her cheek, "Anything for you."

She blinks herself out of a trance, and quickly makes her way to the bathroom to rinse the brushes leaving me standing there in wonder.

The more time we've spent together, the closer we have become. Each day she shares an extra piece of herself. Our days have been filled with laughter and jokes, settling into a comfortable routine topped with nightly movies. I'm hyperaware of her presence- her stares, the effect of her voice, the casual way she drapes her feet over my lap.

I know she's caught me looking, unable to tear my gaze away. Her quiet humming that I'm not sure even she notices, the way her eyes crease when she throws her head back to laugh. My self-restraint continues to thin, which is beginning to become a problem.

She deserves more, and I can't give her that.

Water boiling over grabs my attention. "Shit." Grumbling as some of the hot liquid pours into the sink.

She's going to be the reason I burn the house down.

Interrupting my thoughts, Rain runs up behind me to the sauce that I failed to notice is boiling. Before she can reach it, it explodes splattering all over the walls and ceiling. Sauce saturates our clothes. Shock paints her face as she turns to look at me. The mess drips from her hair. We both break the silence by erupting into a fit of laughter. A drop from the ceiling runs down my face, which causes her to laugh even harder. Instinctively, my arms wrp around her swinging her around in the air determined to keep that heavenly sound flowing out of her. Setting her down she giggles as we regain our breaths. I look down to see her staring at me with a look I haven't seen before. She quickly averts her eyes and backs away as she grabs the mop and rags from the closet leaving a trail of footsteps causing me to chuckle. Carefully grabbing the handle, I sling the half-empty pot of sauce into the sink as the rag, already on the counter, swipes over the cabinets. She returns with her arms filled with what seems like every towel she owns.

My hands are swiping everything out of her hers. "Go get a shower. I've got this."

"Are you sure?"

Looking at her dramatically from head to toe, "Absolutely."

She laughs, "Fine. Can you pick us out a movie, please?" smiling over her shoulder.

How can I say no to that?

She hops as she removes her socks to avoid tracking everything into the rest of the house. They fly through the air as she throws them into the washing machine. Shaking my head, I return to cleaning until the kitchen is spotless again.

The noodles were somehow spared in the chaos. Thinking of the new recipe I was planning on making her, my stubbornness overtakes my defeat. The jar of sauce stares back at me. As it warms in the pot, it takes all of my strength to not let my mind wonder back to the feeling of her in my arms even if it was only for an instant.

Placing the finishing touches on the new recipe, I scoop out enough pasta for both of us. Carefully balancing both plates and both drinks, mindful of every step, I set everything down, doing as I'm told for once as the movies begin scrolling across the screen while I attempt to pick the perfect one.

SHADOWS AND DECEPTION

Chapter Fourteen

Rain

My feet meet the coolness of the tile on my
bare feet. The man in the kitchen invades
my thoughts. Trying to preserve my last
shred of dignity, my head shakes as my
clothes slip off. The water scorches my skin as the shower door
closes behind me. My eyes close, and electric blue eyes flash in my
mind as the warmth of the water continues to engulf me. The
soreness of my stomach from laughing so hard gains my attention
unable to remember the last time that happened. The memories of
a few minutes ago make my body heat.

The thought of seeing the gentle side of him, the human side, paired with those gray sweatpants that failed at hiding what's underneath instantly makes my core ache. With a mind of their own, my hands work their way up. Pinching my left nipple as my other hand slides down to my clit, moving in slow circles, makes me let out a low moan. Despite knowing I need to be quiet, I can't help it when he enters my mind. Speeding up, my fingers slide inside, pumping in and out. Letting my mind wonder what it would feel like to have him inside me. I squeeze my nipple harder, feeling myself tense around my fingers, moving them faster until I explode, moaning. My legs shake. My cum coats my fingers. My back touches the wet tile, attempting to catch my breath. That's the fastest I've ever finished, especially with just images of him playing in my mind.

Reality returns and I can't believe that just happened. He's staying here- in my house. I can't let myself think of him like that. He's just staying here because he needs a place while he heals. I've been in here too long already. Quickly finishing my shower, the towel wraps around me. As the cool air quickly turns my skin to ice, opting for sweatpants and a hoodie tonight.

Chapter Fifteen

Ghost

I'm speechless. Absolutely speechless.

My shoulders drop as the tension leaves at the memory of her laugh. Desperate to hear more, to be the reason for the sound that consumes me. Knowing better than to think of Rain that way, my head shakes away the thoughts- or at least attempts to. Hearing something that gets my attention, my pants almost burst at the seams. Her moans fill my ears.

Oh. My. God.

That's it. My self-restraint is hanging on by a thread. It's the only thing keeping me from going in there. A few minutes later, the water shuts off. I adjust myself before the sound of footsteps fill the hallway.

Looking up, Rain glows as she walks into the living room. An audible gulp sounds, unable to remove the images of what she would look like making those sounds for me out of my head. Dinner is forgotten as she raises a brow at me. Sitting in her spot on the couch, she reaches forward to grab both of our plates. She holds my plate out to me as she studies the TV. With a nod of approval, we start the movie. We both end up eating enough that we can't breathe.

After a few minutes, her feet, once again, end up on my lap. My thumb mindlessly traces circles on the top of her foot.

Opening my eyes, I notice we have fallen asleep on this couch every night since I've been here.

That can't be comfortable for her.

Taking her in, her hoodie slid up, showing a sliver of skin, which is just enough to make my imagination run wild.

Oh boy.

I gently lift her feet and set them down.

Heading to the bathroom, my want for the goddess lying in the other room is unavoidable. Stepping into the shower, the freezing water still doesn't deter my thoughts. That still doesn't help. Closing my eyes, my hand wraps around my cock. My hand moves up and down at the thought of what her pussy feels like- so tight. The images of her legs around my waist while showing her just how badly I want her flash in my mind causing a groan to escape. Pumping faster, tingling starts at my toes working its way up my body.

Faster and faster until my cum coats the tile wall. My hands brace myself against the wall as air attempts to enter my lungs.

I need her.

SHADOWS AND DECEPTION

Chapter Sixteen
Rain

Ringing jostles around in my brain only to realize it's my phone. Groaning, I pull it off of the end table.

Squinting one eye open, "Hey Cass," a yawn suddenly escapes me.

"Hey, gum drop! So I need your ass up and at it this morning. We're going shopping."

"I'm always awake at this hour. Now, do you mind telling me why we need to go shopping?" rolling my eyes.

"We're going to The Hideaway tomorrow, duh."

"After the situation your shoes were almost in last time, you still want to go?" unable to keep the giggle from escaping.

"I'm choosing to ignore that comment. Thank you very much. We just haven't been out together in a while. I miss you."

"You sure are convincing. I miss you, too. I'll meet you at the mall in an hour."

A squeal erupts from the speaker, "You're the best."

She hangs up before anything can come out. Rolling my eyes, the footsteps coming down the hallway gain my attention. Looking up to meet Ghost's eyes, an idea pops into my head.

"Is Ace single?" I blurt out as a hint of jealousy washes over his face.

"Yes, why?" drawing out the question.

Deciding to draw out his torture just a little longer, "Oh, I was just wondering since I wanted someone to take me out tomorrow-"

"No," he cuts in.

Looking up at him from under my lashes, "But, why not?"

Without hesitation, "I'm taking you wherever you want to go. I don't share," flames come out of his eyes at the thought.

A giggle escapes me, "Since when did you decide I was yours?"

Ignoring the question, "Where do you want to go?" He sits on the edge of the couch, puts on his shoes, and looks around frantically for what I assume are his wallet and keys.

Gently placing a hand on his shoulder, unable to hide the smile on my face, "Hold on, cowboy, I'm just teasing you. Cassi and I were planning on going shopping in about an hour. I was wondering if you would like to come with us. Plus, I think Ace would be good for her."

He releases a breath as his body relaxes, "You know you should've started with that."

He grips my chin and studies my face, slowly rubbing his thumb over my lower lip. My eyes don't leave his despite feeling like I'm under a microscope.

He drops his hand as he stands, "Tell me where we're going, and I'll let Ace know," avoiding my eyes.

Did I do something wrong?

Glancing at the mirror above the entry table, quick to avert my gaze. Ace's voice meets my ears as my shoes slide on, "Why the hell would I want to go shopping? Seriously, have you met me?"

Ghost chuckles, "I'll meet you there. Don't forget to look presentable."

He rolls his eyes as Ace hangs up on him. His eyes trail over my body, giving me whiplash from earlier.

He clears his throat, "You look beautiful."

Feeling a blush creep up my neck, "Thank you." Quickly turning to walk out the door before he sees.

Reaching for the car door, my hand pauses as a much larger hand beats me to it. He opens it, nodding for me to get in. He slides in the driver seat with the steering wheel in his chest and his knees crammed on either side.

"What the fuck? Again, really?" he whispers to himself.

Leaning back, laughing, "I didn't know you would be driving earlier, or I would've moved the seat back."

Pinning me with a look that only makes me laugh harder, he slowly backs the seat up. Rolling his eyes, he throws a hand over the back of my seat as he backs up. The music rattles the speakers as the windows roll down, welcoming a breeze. My hair will be a mess by the time we get there, but I don't care. A peaceful sigh escapes my lips. Glancing over, he's smiling with his hand out the window, flowing in sync with the wind. My breath catches while attempting to burn this memory in my mind.

Pulling up at the mall, we scour one aisle after another until Cassi's car gets my attention, surprisingly already parked beside Ace's truck. Leaning against the trunk, Ace rolls his eyes as Cassi animatedly tells a story.

"Would you look at that?" looking over to see a surprised look on his face.

This may go better than we had initially hoped for. As they spot us, they immediately back away from each other.

Pulling into a parking spot near them, "Wait," he holds up a hand, causing my eyebrows to draw together. Ghost walks around the car, opens the door for me, and offers his hand. Taking it as he "helps" me out hesitating to let go. It's our turn to have curious glances thrown our way.

"Ready?" unable to contain her energy, Cassi starts toward the door, expecting us to follow, which we reluctantly do.

"This would look perfect on you!" she squeals, holding up a crimson dress with an open back and deep V neckline.

It's not too fancy, but it will show off all my curves.

"He won't be able to keep his hands off of you." She's bouncing on the balls of her feet at this point, seemingly about to explode.

"I don't know what you're talking about."

She pins me with a stare, knowing without a doubt that I'm lying.

"Fine, give it here." I snatch the dress and haul it into the dressing room. My life flashes before my eyes, almost tripping as it slides on. Luckily, the wall braced my fall.

"You okay in there?" Cassi yells.

"Yes, I'm perfectly fine."

After getting it zipped on the side, my gaze travels down, taking in the dress. The door clicks as it unlocks. My steps falter as I step out into the bright white dressing room, moving to stand in front of the full-length mirror.

A gasp sounds from behind me. "That's perfect! See, I told you."

Running my hands down the front, I realize she's right. "It pains me to say this, but I have to agree," as a smile spreads across my face.

Making my way back and changing into my clothes safely is a success.

"Make sure they aren't by the door. I don't want him to see it until I put it on when we go."

"Turn around and don't look!" she yells at the guys.

Ace grumbles as Ghost laughs. My heart melts a little more.

Hanging up the dress, wiggling my eyebrows at Cassi, "Your turn."

A look of confusion takes over, "You're going to do the same with Ace. Now, go try this on."

Shoving the black dress into her arms, she stumbles into the dressing room. She walks out a minute later, sporting the dress that's fitted with spaghetti straps. The black dress makes her green eyes pop along with her pin straight black hair. She takes in her appearance as her eyes light up.

"It's my turn to tell you I told you so."

Rolling her eyes, "Fine. You were right. There, I said it." Shaking her head, she turns back to the dressing room and changes.

My head peeks out to ensure nobody sees us as we walk up to check out. As soon as our dresses are placed in bags, I feel his eyes on me.

A shiver runs through me, hearing, "Are you trying to leave without us, little bird?"

"No, now go away. You both can't see these until we're ready to go out."

Cassi whips her head around as Ace lets out a scoff.

Narrowing her eyes, "Problem?"

He folds his arms over his chest. Tipping his head back, "No, ma'am."

As we walk back through the parking lot, his phone starts ringing. Ghost grabs it and looks at the screen.

Sighing, "Hey, you, okay?" Only able to hear bits and pieces, I hear him mumble, "Is it okay if I bring someone?"

My curiosity peaks.

He surely can't be talking about me.

The corner of his mouth rises. " I love you too. I'll see you tonight." He turns, noticing the curiosity painted on my face. A smug look takes over his face. "Jealous?"

"Absolutely not," turning my head to look forward, opening the car door before he can.

Staring out the window, he lets out a deep chuckle beside me. My head snaps toward him, and my eyes narrow.

He throws both hands up in surrender. "Go ahead and be jealous of my sister, who, by the way, you're meeting tonight."

My mouth drops. "There is no way I'm meeting your sister tonight. Nope. Not happening."

Backing out, "Oh yes, you are. Besides, she'll love you."

I scoff. "If she hates me, it's your fault."

SHADOWS AND DECEPTION

Chapter Seventeen

Rain

Pulling into the driveway, he opens the door caging me in and grips my chin between his fingers as he looks into my eyes, "Only I open your doors for you. Got it?" Nodding my head, he leans closer and runs his thumb down my lip. My head tilts ever so slightly, wrapping my mouth around his thumb and circling it with my tongue.

Worth a shot.

His eyes widen as he watches the movement. I glance down to see him harden in his jeans. My eyes meet his, determined not to look away. His other hand, beginning at my waist, trails up. He stops as he circles my nipple through my shirt. An involuntary moan leaves my lips. As soon as it does, he pinches it, causing me to gasp. He rubs it to soothe the pain. Suddenly, his hand is wrapped around my throat, slowly tightening. He's barely touching me, and I'm soaked. His voice comes out deep, as if he's trying to keep some amount of control.

"Get in the damn house unless you want the neighbors to watch you get fucked right here. Do you want them to watch as you cum?"

My head shakes, "Good girl. That's only for me to see, and you're about to cum so many times you beg me to stop."

A grin covers my face as my hand reaches for the bulge in his pants.

He tightens his grip around me as he grinds out, "In the house. Now. I want you naked on your bed when I get in there."

Batting my eyelashes at him, "Yes, sir."

He throws his head back as he runs a hand down his face. My hips sway on my way to the door.

Forgive me, Father, for I am going to sin.

Any sense of bravery has completely vanished. Yes, I want him completely, but the nerves are beginning to take over. Still, I all but rip my clothes off. Crawling onto the bed and deciding to lie on my stomach facing the door, the front door slams shut, causing the walls to shake.

Oh boy.

The outline of his figure appears in the doorway, taking me in.

"I changed my mind," seriousness coating his voice.

My heart drops. My hands grip the blankets, pulling them off the bed to cover myself. He's beside my bed in three strides, grabbing a handful of my hair yanking it back toward himself.

Dropping the blanket and sitting up on my knees, his breath dances down my neck, "You better believe I'm still going to fuck you until you cry, but I don't want you on the bed right now."

He pulls my hair, making me stand up. He lets go as he sits on the edge of the bed, taking in my body. "Bend over my knees," he says. I hesitate as I bend over.

He puts his hand on my back, "If you want to stop at any time, tell me. Understand?

Looking back with lust-filled eyes, "Yes."

"Are you on birth control?"

Nodding again, I jolt forward as his hand lands on my ass, certain it left a handprint. "This is for wearing those damn shorts all the time when I wasn't allowed to touch you," smack. "This is for making me want you when I shouldn't," smack. "And this is for the attitude outside that snapped my composure." He dives two fingers in my pussy.

My head falls as a mix of moans and whimpers leave me. He moves his fingers in and out, going faster and faster until my vision starts to fade.

I explode, "Oh God, Ghost!"

He keeps going despite the heightened sensitivity until my second orgasm causes my body to vibrate. Suddenly, he removes his fingers, grabs my shoulder, and forces me down on my knees. "Suck these clean. Taste where my fingers have been."

Opening my mouth and sticking my tongue out, he shoves them in, making me gag as spit runs down my chin and tears leave my eyes.

He smiles down at me, "Good girl. Choke on them." Gargled noises come from my throat.

I can only imagine what his cock will feel like.

He yanks me up by the hair again and tosses me back on the bed. Taking his belt off, he wraps it around my wrists, somehow keeping them tied to the headboard. Still wanting more, his eyes trail down as my legs spread open. He pulls his shirt off with his pants following.

"Do you want me to fuck you with my tongue, little bird, or do you want me to suck on that clit?"

Feeling myself leak down my legs, "Both, please," as a whimper leaves my mouth.

"Good girl. I'm going to worship every inch of this body, and you're going to take it," not taking his eyes off me.

Throwing my legs over his shoulders, he dives right in before my brain can catch up to what's happening— licking and sucking until I feel his tongue enter me, just like he said. My head falls back. He looks up, not moving his mouth away from me, and returns to what he was doing. My legs tighten around him.

"Please," I draw out, "Please, I need you inside of me."

"Beg."

"Please, please, please fuck me," almost to the verge of tears.

His eyes darken as he rises to his knees. He pins my legs as far back as they'll go as he lines himself up. Rubbing himself over my slit, my legs already feel like Jello.

"Please, Ghost. I need you."

He looks me in the eyes, "My name is Greyson. When you scream while I make you cum over and over, that better be what I hear."

I nod my head as my eyes trail down to watch as he enters me. He begins slowly, his eyes never leaving my face. They slowly travel down my body as his hand makes its way up. His hand meets my neck as his fingers slowly dig into my flesh, still allowing me to breathe, but firm enough to keep me in place. He begins thrusting faster and faster as my breasts move with every movement. He leans down, takes a nipple in his mouth, and bites down. His hand never leaves my throat. Every sensation amplifies as a scream escapes. He does the same to the other side. Leaning back with a smirk. He throws his head back, groaning as I squeeze around him. Looking back up, he forces a thumb in my mouth, forcing me to suck. He removes it, pressing it directly on my clit. The orgasm rips through me as my eyes roll back. He follows soon, filling me up until his cum drips out.

He leans forward as we both attempt to slow our breathing and presses a gentle kiss against my lips before standing to walk toward the bathroom. My body goes limp before his footsteps return to the bed. He gently opens my legs and cleans me with a warm washcloth. A small smile appears on my face. He leans over, removing the belt, pausing to kiss my lips. He lays beside me as he wraps an arm around me, pulling me close. His entire body relaxes as he runs a hand through my hair.

"I'm in deep with you, little bird."

"Me too," running a hand over his chest. "Why do they call you Ghost?"

He runs his hand down his face, tugging me closer with his other. "I'll tell you one day."

Chapter Eighteen

Ghost

"I'm going to get a shower before we have to go."

Shopping took way longer than expected. Especially since it was an absolute must to stop at every shoe store we saw, according to Cassi.

Something is going on between her and Ace. I just know it.

Adding in what Rain and I finally gave into, that has officially made us late. My eyes land on her as I walk out of the kitchen. Quickly turning on her heels, she goes down the hallway to the bathroom. The fact that she can make me feel this way without laying a finger on me isn't normal- not at all.

Opening the door, she's coating her lips with lipstick. My eyes close as my arms wrap around her, inhaling the scent that is now my comfort- taking in the woman who is now my comfort.

"You look beautiful, little bird." Turning her around and placing a gentle kiss on her forehead.

Looking up with her big brown eyes that remind me of the coffee I need to function every morning, she meets my eyes, "And you look very handsome." She leans up and places a kiss on my lips.

"Are you ever going to tell me why you call me that?"

"One day," I let go and walk out, "You coming?" I yell, standing next to the door.

She comes out, attempting to walk and put heels on at the same time causing a chuckle to escape me. My hand catches her arm as she stumbles laughing. Each time I hear it, I know heaven must be real.

My angel. My savior. My little bird.

Once she straightens, we're out the door.

Chapter Nineteen

Rain

As we pull in, the sight before me is overwhelming. In the middle of hundreds of empty acres sits a breathtaking white two-story house with a wraparound porch and flowers framing the front. My mouth drops.

Grinning, "Are you ready to meet the family?"

I feel like I'm going to puke.

"Absolutely."

He comes around to open my door, offering his hand to help me out. He never lets go, causing my nerves to settle ever so slightly. He bangs on the door once as it swings open. A man who's no older than 35 appears. His blonde hair seems deliberately messy, paired with dark brown eyes. What looks like a small cotton ball runs down the hallway, ignoring Ghost and jumps up on my leg.

"Oh my goodness! I'm in love. Who is this little fluff ball?" I can't help but squeal, picking it up as it licks my face.

Looking over, Ghost and River are staring at us in shock.

"What?" I say between giggles as I pet behind the little angel's ears.

"That's-that's my dog, Snowball." He stutters out.

"This is Snowball? Can she come home with us, please?" I beg.

He finally closes his mouth, "I think she's already made that decision for us."

Snowball nuzzles into his hand as he reaches to scratch behind her ears. His eyes roam over my face as the corners of his mouth turn up.

"I'm River. You the one that's been taming this guy?" reaching his hand out with a giant smile.

Some of my nerves start to dissipate. Reaching out, "I'm Rain. I'm at least trying to," glancing up to toss a wink at Ghost.

River throws his head back, laughing, "She's good for you. Come on in. Lil's in the kitchen."

The nerves are back in full force.

Walking into the kitchen, a woman with shoulder length black hair has her back to us while stirring something in a bowl.

Once she hears us enter, she turns around, beaming. "You must be the one my brother won't shut up about."

Blushing, I sneak a glance up at Ghost as he shoots daggers at her. She rolls her eyes as she comes forward, holding her arms out. She doesn't wait for the same response as her arms wrap around me. My arms automatically wrap around her.

She leans back and keeps her hands on my shoulders. "You are gorgeous!"

Unable to withhold a giggle, "Thank you, I'm Rain. It's really nice to meet you."

"I'm Lily, Ghost's favorite sister."

"You're my only sister, Lil," he mumbles.

Ignoring him, "Anyway, sit down and tell me about yourself. River, will you take Ghost in there with you? This is girl talk," motioning her hand toward the hallway.

He laughs, "Yes, dear. Come on, let's go," placing a hand on Ghost's shoulder.

He looks back, giving me a reluctant look as River leads him away.

Turning back to see Lily still smiling, "What?" I giggle.

"He's just never brought a woman over for me to meet. Anyway, tell me how you met."

"Oh dear," placing a hand over my face." Well, I'm a nurse in the ER over in Willbrook. I ended up walking into a room with him waiting, involuntarily, I should mention. Long story short, I ended up waiting with his friends while he was in the hospital and offered him a place to stay while he's healing."

Looking up to see she's standing before me with the whisk by her side and her mouth hanging open.

"What?"

"You mean to tell me his friends didn't tell you to leave, and he let you stay with him in the hospital?"

"Yeah, why?

"A. he never lets anyone see him when he isn't 100%, and B. his friends don't like anyone. They're extremely close so they don't let many people in."

"Why are they so close?" causing my eyebrows to draw together.

Realizing she isn't stirring, she grabs the bowl and continues facing me, "You should ask him about that." A soft smile forms.

"Well, now it's your turn. I want to know all about his favorite sister," smiling as the nerves begin to settle.

"We were always really close growing up. I've always known he would be there if I needed him. Hell, he was there even when I didn't. We didn't have the best childhood, but also something for him to share. Anyway, he made it better." She stares off, lost in thought. Shaking her head, "When I was eight, our mom left me on the steps of the police station the same day our dad died. She told me to stay right there, and she would be back. As you can guess, she never was. After a couple of hours, an officer found me holding an old stuffed teddy bear that used to be Ghost's. I ended up in state custody landing in a group home."

Gasping, "That's terrible, Lily. I'm so sorry."

"I'm not complaining. That's actually how I met River," smiling at the memory. "That's another story, but we ended up having Jax, who is currently using Ghost as his personal playground." She leans over peeking through the doorway.

Following her gaze, I lean over, seeing Jax climbing over his shoulder. Ghost stands up with an arm around him, spinning around as he does. Laughter fills the air. An enormous smile covers both of their faces while River is holding his stomach, laughing on the couch. He feels our stares as his eyes instantly meet mine. Lily and I both snap back out of sight, giggling like kids who have been caught with their hands in the cookie jar. She turns around and faces the counter. She pours the mix into a glass pan and places it in the oven. Turning back, she braces both hands on the counter as she studies me.

"Can I ask you something?"

Her gaze lands back on me, "Of course. Ask away."

"Did you ever see your mom again?"

"Once. I was getting on the city bus to make it back to the group home before curfew. I had just taken a seat when I saw a woman walking. I knew she looked just like my mother. I pretty much bolted out the door, attempting to chase her down. As I got older, I had a lot of anger toward her. Never understanding why she left me there on those steps," shaking her head. "I ended up losing her in the crowd. Plus, I missed curfew as well. I have to admit that's not the best day I've ever had. What about your family?"

My lips turn down. She notices the movement, "You don't have to say anything if you don't want to."

"You've shared your story with me. My dad disappeared when I was younger leaving my mom and me. I ended up taking care of her until I was 18, when I finally had to place her in Rosewood," shame fills my body.

"Come on mom, get in the car."

She finally made it out of bed and down the stairs.

"No, Rain. You know I don't want to go out."

"Just this once, please,"

She looks into my eyes.

I look away as guilt overtakes me.

"Fine." She slowly opens the door, her eyes widening as if waiting for something to jump out.

She makes her way to the car. Once she sits down, she refuses to look in my direction.

She stares straight ahead until she realizes where we're going. "What do you think we're doing here?"

We pull up in front of an old mansion that has since been turned into Rosewood Mental Institution. Turning to look at her, a tear runs down her face.

"You need help, Mom."

Two employees come out. One opens her door as the other stands to the side. Pure rage takes over her features. "You bitch!" she lunges, attempting to sink her claws into my face.

I jerk back, failing to recognize the woman in front of me.

The woman who would make me peanut butter sandwiches. The woman who was supposed to love me.

Hands reach out, gripping her arms. They drag her out as she begins kicking and screaming, "I'm going to fucking kill you. You're dead to me, Rain! Dead to me!" The sliding glass doors close, causing her voice to fade.

My forehead meets the steering wheel as a sob escapes me. I had no other choice. She was rotting away in the bed.

She needs help.

Bringing me back to the present, "Hey, there's nothing wrong with that. It sounds like she clearly needed help. It's a great thing you were able to realize that, especially as young as you were."

"She did, without a doubt. For a long time, I held a lot of anger toward her. I guess I still do. I had to work two jobs and go to school. I know it wasn't her fault, but she just gave up. I was struggling, too. I practically lost both of my parents at the same time."

Pausing as I meet her eyes, I whisper, "You did, too."

She nods, "I did. I was in a similar situation where I was angry. After I met River, I saw what a healthy relationship looked like. Once we had Jax, I made it my mission not to turn into my parents. I wanted him to be happy and healthy and surrounded by love—surrounded by things Ghost and I were never able to experience."

I nod in understanding.

The moment disappears as Jax runs in laughing, "Mom! Did you see me? Did you see me? I climbed all the way up to Uncle Ghost's shoulders!"

His excitement is contagious. I can't help but giggle at the little boy.

He runs across the kitchen, grabbing my hands, continuing to hop up and down. "Did you see me, too?"

"Yes, I did. That was amazing!" matching his energy.

I peek around the corner to see Ghost watching his sister and me. His gaze quickly changes to focus on the little boy running back to him. Jax's legs are bent, and arms are out as he prepares to tackle him onto the couch.

Turning back to Lily, "Have you always been close to each other?"

A frown graces her lips as her gaze flickers between her family and me. "Once I was placed in the group home, I lost contact with him. It broke my heart every single day knowing he wasn't there. I tried over the years to find him, but I never could. Eventually, River came home one evening describing a man he worked with. It sounded just like my brother. River knew the history, so when I asked to meet him, he didn't hesitate to agree. That evening, I made dinner. If it wasn't my brother, I at least wanted the man to have something to eat at the end of the night."

A hint of a smile appears. "My nerves were shot the closer I came to meeting him. When I opened the door and saw him standing there, I knew that it was my brother looking back at me. We've been inseparable ever since."

At that moment, the timer decides to go off. She whips around, grabbing two potholders. Opening the oven, steam pours from the cake in the glass dish. The scent fills the air with the faint smell of chocolate. The dish barely touches the counter as a blur flies past.

"Can I have a bite, mom? Please," he draws out.

She chuckles, "It's still hot, Jax, plus you need to eat dinner first."

"Ugh. Fine."

He rounds the corner, heading to the dining room. The feeling of a hand travels up the back of my neck, gently tugging my hair back, forcing my eyes to meet ice-blue ones staring down at me. He releases it as he places a kiss on my temple, straightening back up. Lily's face shows a glimpse of a smile as she quickly turns back around.

Now, it's going to be awkward. Great.

Ghost walks past, grabbing dishes filled with every food you can imagine, and returns to the dining room.

"I've never seen him genuinely happy, especially that happy." She throws a quick glance my way.

"I think I could say the same about myself."

"Good. You two seem good for each other."

Do we? What if he doesn't want anything serious? What if I'm overthinking everything?

Changing the subject, "Where are the plates? I'll go set the table."

"They're in the cabinet beside me. Thank you."

I walk to the giant wooden table with a handful of plates, inhaling the scent as a rainbow of food covers the surface. River walks in, holding Jax over his shoulder, causing everyone to laugh.

Conversation flows between us as if we've all known each other forever. Snowball has decided to lie underneath my chair, refusing to move a muscle.

"Thank you for having me over. I had an amazing time-" Before the sentence can leave my mouth, a little boy appears, gripping my legs with both arms.

"Can you come back sometime? I really like you. Uncle Ghost really likes you, too," chuckles fill the air.

Turning to glance up at Ghost, he answers for me, "She'll be back, buddy. I promise." A warm smile spreads across his face as he looks down at me.

Lily grabs me in a hug next, "Seriously, come back anytime. Have him send you my number."

Ghost interrupts, "Come on, it's getting late."

"Goodnight, everyone!" letting Ghost lead me to the car.

Chapter Twenty
Ghost

As silence fills the car, I wonder what she and my sister spoke about. Glancing over, Rain looks out the passenger window with Snowball in her lap as we pull into the driveway, deep in thought.

On instinct, my hand reaches over automatically, intertwining our fingers and rubbing circles on the back of her hand. "What are you thinking so hard about?" My eyes bounce between the road and her face. She meets my eyes.

"Well. Um-" she stutters.

"Hey, I promised you could ask me anything, and I'll tell you the truth. If you have questions, ask," offering a comforting smile.

"I have a few if that's okay," chewing on her lip.

"Of course, go ahead."

"Why did Lily end up in foster care? What happened to you? Why are you and the guys so close?"

He comes barreling at me with everything he has. He's a mountain of a man, while I haven't exactly hit my growth spurt yet. The next thing I know, my back hits the floor. My head is spinning, and my mother's screams are barely audible as I try to free myself from the blackness threatening to take hold of my vision. Wait, out of my peripheral, my eyes lock onto something peeking out from under the table as the sunlight hits it. Trying to move over ever so slightly has proven difficult with this monster of a man still on top of me. As he raises his fist to swing again with all of his strength, an empty beer bottle crashes into the side of his head. Instantly, blood begins to drip down his face, landing on mine. He falls to the side. Shoving his body off of mine, my legs are finally under me again as I stand. Holding onto the wall, a wave of nausea hits me in full force. Thankfully, it's under control. Unsure if he's still alive, I quickly grab a bag and stuff it with everything that will fit. This won't happen again. Nobody will touch me again. Never.

My eyes widen at the sight of my mother running out of the front door, dragging my sister behind her. She never looked back. She was free, which was all that mattered to her at the moment—not the son she left behind. Looking back over my shoulder, he still hasn't moved.

Oops.

116

I feel nothing. Promising myself, this is the last time I'll ever look back. Walking into my new life, one foot in front of the other. Away from a raging alcoholic father, away from the beatings, and away from the daily torture of being stuck with no way out. Never again.

Inhaling a deep breath, "Listen, I'll tell you with complete transparency, I'm a monster—a devil in disguise. I don't want your opinion of me to change. I care about you, Rain- more than I should."

"I care about you, too. I want to know the monster, not just the man that will fight off my demons for me."

"When we were young, my dad was an abusive drunk. The more he would drink, the harder he would hit," shaking my head. "He tried to go after my mom and Lily, but most of the time, I would piss him off enough to become the target of his rage."

"No," she whispers.

Squeezing her hand, "When I was 15, he tried to go after her again. Something in me snapped. I lost every shred of self-control when he hit me. My only focus was on protecting my mom and sister. I ended up killing the piece of shit that night." Terrified to see her reaction, I squeeze my eyes shut. Feeling her pull her hand away causes a wave of pain to crash over me. Immediately, the feeling vanishes as I feel her hands on my face. Reluctantly looking up, the tears flow down her face.

"You are not a monster. You adapted to your surroundings to survive." Her thumb rubs under my eyes, wiping away the tears. Unaware they were running down my face.

"You were never given the chance to be a child. You were forced into a role to protect. Never think less of yourself for doing what you had to do."

Turning my head, my lips connect to the inside of her palm. She removes them and returns to holding each hand.

Clearing my throat, "That leads to another story."

"I want to know whatever you're willing to share."

"I told you, you're mine. I mean that so you deserve to know," looking down at our hands, "after he was killed, my mom took Lily and never looked back. I was left alone but refused to stay in that house. I didn't want to be haunted by the past anymore. Friends were non-existent growing up, so sleeping in alleyways became normal until a man found me one night."

"He took me in. It had snowed all evening. I probably would've died if he hadn't. I think at that point, I wished for it- an end to the pain and guilt. When he took me in, Luke was already staying there. We all have similar backgrounds, unfortunately. That's probably what made us so close in the beginning. After being there for about six months, Ace came along. For a long time, it was just us. About a year later, Cam came along. The man who took us in, East, taught us to be loyal, protective, and truthful no matter the situation. We had all learned how to keep our demons at bay. When Cam showed up, he was different. He still had a sliver of positivity. We saw hope in him, so we chipped in and attempted to teach him everything we had learned ourselves."

Pausing, taking a deep breath, "East got wrapped up with the wrong people. He started turning us into monsters. They'd hire us to kill, to get information, anything you could ask for. He, of course, got every dime from it. Compared to some of the things that happened in our childhoods, all of those things didn't seem that bad. We tried to keep Cam from the worst of it as much as possible. One afternoon, he had me perched on a roof, waiting for a target. I was leaning down, looking through the scope, taking everything in, when I saw Lily bolt off a city bus and run down the sidewalk. That was the first time I had seen her since we were separated. I never figured out what she was chasing after. At that moment, I decided enough was enough and walked away. I stayed in the shadows a lot. No matter where I went or what I did, I never left any tracks. That's why they call me Ghost. Nobody could ever prove I was there."

Looking over, Rain's mouth has fallen open as tears flow. "That was the past, little bird. I'm thankful I left when I did. Once I left the city that day, the guys and I were able to break away after I explained to them what had happened. The situation only got worse after we left. Now, we still work together but only take jobs for the right reasons."

Nodding, "Thank you for trusting me with that. You all were so young, and to be forced into that position is mind-blowing." Silence fills the car. I can feel the thoughts flowing through her mind.

"I guess it's my turn now," taking in a deep breath. "A year after my mom left, when I was 19, I met a man that I thought I loved. It was amazing at first, but it slowly started to change. First, there were snide comments here and there, followed by him not wanting to touch me because my body had changed. He played off of my insecurities. He would talk to other women about our problems when getting him to open up to me was nearly impossible. I was in tears one night because he had pushed me and pushed me emotionally. He ended up getting in my face saying, 'You stupid bitch'."

My teeth clench as my hands curl into fists. Nobody should ever be made to feel that way.

"That was the moment I decided I had enough. The next morning, while he was at work, I packed up everything that would fit in my car, and I left. I never looked back. But that was three years ago. I've had time to move on from it. The things he said still play in the back of my mind daily."

"I promise you will never have to worry about that again. I'll prove that to you every single day."

We both take a moment to let everything that was said sink in.

She breaks the silence, "I saw you that night, you know."

There's no way. No one ever sees me. I'm a Ghost.

"What night?"

"The night Cassi and I were at The Hideaway. I could feel your eyes on me. The feeling of someone behind me stopped when I glanced back and didn't see you. I nearly missed the car seat because I saw that you were back. For some reason, even with blood on your hands, I knew you wouldn't hurt me."

Taking everything in, my eyes meet hers, "You asked why I call you little bird?"

"Yes," she turns, waiting for an explanation.

"When I saw you that night, your laugh is what initially got my attention. You just seemed so free, and I wanted more."

She lights up, "No one's ever noticed me in that way before." Her face takes on a serious expression. "I need you to promise me something."

"Of course. Anything."

"Never hide from me again."

"I promise, little bird."

She reaches her pinky in front of my face like it's an official agreement.

"Pinky promise."

SHADOWS AND DECEPTION

Chapter Twenty-One

Rain

"You better be ready when I get there. I'm ten minutes away."

"Would you calm down, Cass," unable to stop the smile as anticipation runs through me. "I'll be ready. Let me know when you're here."

"I'll come in there and drag you out if you aren't," grumbling as she ends the call.

The sheer pink lip gloss coats my lips. Fluffing my hair, I attempt to throw heels on without breaking my neck. As the front door opens, headlights instantly blind me. The toe of my shoes catches on the brick lining the walkway, which causes me to fly forward.

Thankfully, I can steady myself before landing in the dirt. Looking up, Cassi is bent over the steering wheel, attempting to catch her breath. Rounding the front of the car, shooting her a death glare that only makes her laugh harder.

Swinging open the passenger door, "Are you done yet?"

She wheezes as she looks up, tears from laughter filling her eyes. "You looked like a baby deer trying to walk!" Another wave of laughter takes over as I involuntarily join in.

"Hey, did you not see the way I saved it? Plus, you know I never wear heels. I'm not used to being this far up off the ground," scooting in the car seat.

We're finally able to get our giggles under control. "You really do look great," throwing a quick glance over my outfit.

"You do too, as always," I tell her, causing her to dramatically flip her hair.

At the last red light about a block away, I look out the window. People have started swarming, moving in the direction of The Hideaway. People dancing, singing, and laughing begins to fill the streets. When the light suddenly turns green, Cassi floors it. Pulling into the parking lot, we realize there isn't a single empty spot.

"Do you mind walking a little bit?" annoyance lacing her tone.

"Nope. You can always carry me like when we were younger, right?" a mischievous grin covers my face.

She snorts, "Yeah, right. You owe me after the number of times I had to carry you out after you had one too many."

"Fine," groaning as we step on the curb, walking in the direction of The Hideaway. The building comes into view as the streetlamp begins to flicker.

They should fix that.

Ignoring it, we continue the hike until we're standing in front of the glass windows littered with fingerprints and smudges. The place is booming. A crowd gathers around the pool table as drinks begin sloshing.

Just like last time.

SHADOWS AND DECEPTION

Chapter Twenty-Two

Ghost

"Our buddy, Tyler, has decided to cooperate more than before. I thought you might like to see him," sounding proud of himself.

"Of course I do," I snap. "Can you come pick me up?"

"Be there in five." He ends the call without waiting for a reply.

Sending Rain a text explaining Ace needs me but to make sure she knows I will be back soon.

The rumble of a truck gets my attention just as my feet slide into my boots. I step out the door, making sure it's locked behind me. She didn't give me a key, but that'll be a problem for later.

After a few minutes of silence, "How are things going staying with Rain? Are you hanging in there?" looking at me with a mischievous grin.

Running my hand through my hair, "I'm falling for her."

A smile creeps onto my face, thinking of her glued to the TV with her mouth full of popcorn, simply being herself.

"It's about time you admitted that fact to yourself. You can't keep the walls up around you forever. We've done a lot of things, but that doesn't mean you shouldn't allow yourself to be happy." Suddenly uncomfortable with the fact that he's right, "So when are you going to ask Cassi out?" A smirk creeps up on my face.

He sputters out, "Well, um, I don't have feelings for her, so why would I? We grew up together, so it would be weird."

Really? That's the best he could come up with?

"Bullshit, just do it already. You put me in the position of staying with Rain and look how that turned out. Come on, do it for me," dramatically batting my eyelashes at him.

He chuckles, "Fine, but she'll probably shoot me down anyway."

We pull up to the house that's away from the chaotic city. Growing more agitated, my heavy steps walk through the metal door once again. The flickering bulb barely shines on the man's face. Looking around the room, Luke and Cam lean against the wall, somehow blending in. They're used to being the ones to keep watch. My eyes take in the man again who's hanging from the metal pipe.

Barely able to grind out, "Spill it. Now."

He stutters, eyes almost bulging out of his head, "I don't know anything. We take orders from some guy. Everyone calls him Big John. He doesn't let anyone see him, though."

Truth shows in his eyes. Roughly grabbing his jaw, my grip tightens, "Tell me about drugging the women. Why that bar?"

He gulps, "It's the most popular one in this part of the city. I go, persuade a woman to try a sip of my drink. Next thing you know, I'm helping her out the back and into the trunk of my car." As he recalls what he does, a sadistic grin spreads across his face. "Most of them look like they would be a good time or at least decent, but Big John doesn't let us touch what's his."

Grinding my teeth, "Where do you take them?"

"Nope, that's all you're getting from me. Good luck with that," letting out a maniacal laugh.

I snap. Without a second thought, my hand is around the knife from the table on my left, swinging it around to pierce the guy's neck. Blood squirts everywhere. Thankfully, I moved back in time before it covers my shirt. Turning around, staring at the floor, and pacing like a caged animal, it takes all my strength to regain any composure I may still possess.

My eyes snap to the men against the wall. "You two. What do you have on him?"

Cam starts bouncing on the balls of his feet as Luke strolls over.

He begins, "Your friend here has an impressive history of sexual assault, battery, and kidnapping charges. It's unsurprising, considering what he's been doing. No friends or family that I could find. He was in and out of rehab several times, but it never did stick." Rubbing a hand through his hair, "Now, this is the interesting part. There's absolutely nothing on this Big John guy. I've looked everywhere and nothing. That's when we found another man we believe is somehow tied to this. Ryan Collins.

"He's a bad guy, Ghost, like really bad." Cam chimes in.

"Send me every detail," I'm barely able to grind out.

A hand on my shoulder stops me as my mind begins to unravel. Looking up, I see Luke staring at me. "Go home to her and try to relax. You're going to give yourself an aneurysm." I nod, closing my eyes.

Where do I know that name from?

Without a word, Ace grabs his keys out of his pocket and heads for the stairs.

With one last look, I follow behind him, sending Rain a quick message to let her know I'm on my way home.

Home?

He pulls up in the driveway. A sigh escapes as thoughts overwhelm my mind. My feet stomp up to the door, fire flowing through my body. Reaching for the handle, it turns with ease as I step in.

Wait, why's it unlocked? I know for a fact it was locked.

Pure terror takes over, "Rain!" my voice shakes.

Barging into her bedroom to see her blankets thrown back. Turning back, the bathroom door is wide open with the light off.

She's not here.

Turning my head as I jog into the living room, Rain stands in the kitchen doorway, wide-eyed and frozen in place. In three strides, I'm standing in front of her, my hands touching every part of her face and working their way down her arms.

She's okay. She's here.

My hands land back on her face, leaning my forehead to hers.

She looks into my eyes, instantly extinguishing the flames threatening to overtake me. "What the hell happened, Greyson?" She runs her eyes over me to make sure I'm in one piece.

"I'm not good for you, Rain. I know that, but you've turned me into a selfish, selfish man."

Without warning, my lips crash down on hers, hands moving to the nape of her neck, gripping a handful of her hair. She lets out a soft moan. My teeth gently bite down on her lip, pulling back. She moves forward, desperate to keep the connection. Her hands have a death grip on my shirt.

"Please," she whispers, "So help me if you stop touching me right now,"

Grinning, I dive back in for more.

Chapter Twenty-Three

Rain

His hands tighten in my hair, his hands trail down my body. He grabs my waist, pulling me as close as possible. It's my turn to bite his lip as he groans. His lips move down my neck, biting and licking. Stepping back, my back hits the wall. He grinds his hips into me.

"Please. Please. Please," I beg.

Feeling him smirk against my skin, one of his hands move my legs around his waist. I'm so wet he can probably feel it through my shorts, but at this moment, I don't care. Clawing at the buttons on his shirt, managing to get three undone before he rips my shirt off, throwing it behind him. His breath catches as he takes in my body. Suddenly, feeling selfconscious, my arms instinctively move up to cover myself. Before they meet my skin, his hands wrap around my wrist in one swift motion, pinning them against the wall. His eyes darken as his free hand jerks my bra down, exposing my breasts. Before I know what's happening, his tongue is swirling around my nipple.

His mouth moves to the other, doing the same thing. Thinking he's going to pull back, he bites my nipple, barely pulling. Throwing my head back, unable to ignore the ache between my legs. One wrist wiggles out of his grip and reaches for the bulge in his pants that's barely being contained.

That poor zipper.

My hand moves up and down, feeling how hard he is. I need him inside me, or I'm going to explode.

Before I can continue, he scoops me up and throws me over his shoulder. Barely able to make out the feeling of him. I begin unbuttoning the rest of his shirt. The door hits the wall as he walks in. Tossing me on the bed, he takes me in from the top of my head to my toes. He crawls on top of me, hovering, continuing the assault on my mouth. When he moves back, I instantly miss the feeling of him. That doesn't last long as he trails his lips down my neck. He pushes my breasts together, sucking and biting. He continues down my body until his breath is on my core.

He looks up mischievously, causing my brows to draw together. "Beg."

Let's make this fun.

My hands run down my body to the inside of my thighs. "Please put your mouth on me, fuck me. I'll be good, I promise."

He throws his head back, groaning. Unzipping his pants, he lets out a sigh of relief. He dives right in, circling and sucking my clit. My back arches off the bed, and my hands reach for his hair. He stops, looking into my eyes with a smug expression, "No touching."

My mouth opens, but before anything can come out, he lifts my hips, driving his tongue into me. Moaning at the feeling of his tongue licking up and down. He doesn't stop until my legs shake as I grip the sheets with all my strength. My orgasm feels like a wave pouring over me. He bites my inner thigh as he leans back, satisfied with his work.

Standing, he looks down at me. "You were such a good girl."

An idea suddenly pops into my head. "I can be better."

He looks at me in confusion as I slide down the edge of the bed. Sitting on my knees, my hands reach forward, pulling his jeans and boxers down at the same time, coming face to face with the zipper's enemy. My eyes drift up to see him once again sporting that smirk. Not breaking eye contact, I lean forward, moving my tongue slowly around the head of his cock, drawing out a loud groan. Without warning, I take as much of him in my mouth as I can. Tears run down my face, but I continue bobbing up and down. His legs tense, but before I can finish my payback, he grabs me under the arms, flipping me on my stomach. A loud smack fills the air as his hand meets my ass.

He pauses, "Are you sure?"

"Yes, please, I need you to touch me," I beg.

He grins as he watches himself slide into me.

I've died and gone to heaven.

He starts slow but begins pumping faster. His hand runs across my skin from my hip until he's rubbing my clit. My toes begin to curl. He growls as my nails scrape down his back.

"Oh God, Greyson!"

My body shakes uncontrollably. After I come down, he pulls out of me. Turning around, an arm wraps me up and turns me over.

"Hold your hands out." Doing as I'm told, he leans down and grabs his belt from the floor. "Good girl" leaves his lips as he wraps it around my wrists like before. He throws my legs over his shoulders as he enters me again. "Fuck woman, you want me to fill this pussy up again?"

"I don't think I can take anymore," I moan.

"You can and you will," he slams into me. Leaning forward, he grabs the belt, pinning my wrists to the bed. He enters me harder and harder. The bed creaks as his panting quickens. "Come for me like a good girl, little bird." I scream as I explode. He continues thrusting into me, hitting my sensitive clit every time, causing my eyes to roll back. My legs shake as he follows me soon after.

Like before, he slips out of me and walks to the bathroom. Without any tension left in my body, his footsteps return only a moment later. He gently opens my legs and cleans me. Looking down, my fingers run gently through his hair. A soft smile graces his face as his eyes meet mine. He presses a gentle kiss on my inner thigh before moving up to my lips. He lays beside me as he wraps an arm around me, pulling me close. His entire body relaxes. He runs a hand through my hair as we let sleep overcome us.

SHADOWS AND DECEPTION

Chapter Twenty-Four

Rain

"No," groaning as the alarm clock blares.

A deep chuckle coming from beside me paired with the arm around my waist tightening, "You know you have to go to work even if I would much rather have you stay here."

"Don't remind me," turning to bury my face in his chest.

Sighing, I raise up and throw my legs over the side of the bed. Looking back over my shoulder, I take in the sight before me- hair pointing in every direction, those dimples paired with the smile that's aimed toward me, with his arms over his head. My eyes, with a mind of their own, begin their way down every inch of skin stopping as the blanket unfortunately stops my enjoyment.

"You won't be leaving this room if you don't stop that," amusement painting his face.

I roll my eyes and pretend I wasn't placing every single detail of him in my long-term memory. Walking to the shower, I stretch my arms above my head stretching every muscle in my body.

The sound of the drain swirling brings me back to the present as I step into the steaming water. I can't help but close my eyes as I lean my head back. The sliding door opens and closes briefly before I feel hands in my hair. I immediately relax even more as my shampoo is massaged into my scalp and covers every strand. I blink away the water droplets on my eyelashes to see Ghost looking down at me with a softness in his eyes that I haven't seen before. I reach up placing my hand on his cheek followed by my lips meeting his. Leaning my head back, the water runs through.

Giggling, "Lean down a little bit."

He leans down and closes his eyes as my fingers run through his hair. I pepper kisses over his face causing a smile to spread across his face. He straightens as he removes every bubble from his hair. After turning the water off, he wraps a fluffy towel around my shoulders. With a towel around his waist, he walks across the room to slip on a pair of sweatpants. The time on the clock grabs my attention as my eyes widen.

I'm going to be late for work.

I finish getting ready to leave when I hear the bedroom door open and close. I throw on my scrubs and run to the kitchen to grab my lunch only to find Ghost standing there with a bag in his hand.

"Go on," he shoves the bag toward me and presses a kiss on my lips.

"Thank you," I scramble out the door to meet the chaos of the day.

I close my eyes taking in a deep breath as I walk through the door, the smell of disinfectant invades my nose along with the all too familiar sounds of beeping and chaos. I hesitate as I make my way to clock in.

Something's different.

My head snaps back to the waiting room taking everyone in. One patient is rocking back and forth staring into oblivion. Baggy clothes hang from her thin frame. Across the room is a man with slick back hair with an obviously tailored suit. His shoes reflect the light overhead. Sprinkled throughout the room, some of them look like they've just left the office whereas others look like they haven't slept in days. All too concerned with their own ailments, nobody seems to have noticed my presence. Shaking my head I continue clocking in and throw my bag in my locker.

Just a little longer.

Making my way around the corner, I run right into a familiar face. "Hey Kate, what are you doing down here?" confusion lacing my voice.

"Oh hey," clearly frazzled "someone called in, so they had me come down here to help," her eyes dart around never exactly meeting mine.

"I just got here, so I'm good to go," attempting a smile but failing.

"Thanks, I'll see you after while." She bolts off before I can respond.

That was strange-.

Before I could finish my thought a scream echoes through the hallway. Running into the room that holds the source of the sound, I'm instantly met with the sight of a young girl lashing out at anyone who dares to come near, her body jerks in unnatural movements.

Bolting to the side of the bed, I take in the girl's features. Beautiful long black hair that has become matted with ivory skin that has now become dull. Her eyes look in my direction, but stare right through me. Dark purple circles surround her eyes. Suddenly feeling the presence of someone behind me, I whip my head around. A woman in her mid-40s, dressed in a white coat, stands there watching the young girl in her own personal hell.

"Aren't you going to help me or just stand there?" I grind out.

She looks from me to the girl and back, lightly nodding her head. She paints a perfect smile on her face, "Oh honey, of course I am."

Goosebumps rise on my skin. After an eternity, the girl is thankfully stable.

I round the corner when the tip of a blade meets my neck. Glancing down, my eyes trace from the hand that's holding it to the body it's attached to. Holding my chin higher, I look directly into the eyes of the woman that I had only met earlier. The white coat is still the same, but her perfectly painted smile has melted off exposing a sneer. Remnants from her red lipstick speckle her teeth.

Met with an unexpected wave of bravery, "What the hell are you doing and what do you want?"

She tilts her head back and cackles sounding like nails on a chalkboard. Her eyes seemed to have turned black.

"What do I want? I want a lot of things. Things that don't pertain to you. But at this moment," pressing the blade into my skin, bringing her lips next to my ear, "I want you to let Ghost know he isn't the only monster that was born that day."

Jerking my head back, "Hold on just a second, how do you know him, and who the hell do you think you are threatening him like that?"

A maniacal grin covers, "I'm sure he'll know. Just make sure he gets the message."

She jerks her hand back, puts the perfect smile back, and simply walks off back through the waiting room and out the front door. After picking my jaw up off the floor, with shaky hands, I'm able to get my phone out of my pocket without dropping it.

He picks up on the second ring, "Miss me already little bird?"

My breathing becomes more forced, closing my eyes in an attempt to slow everything down.

Hearing the hesitation, "What's going on, Rain? I'm on my way. Don't move a muscle. Just breathe, baby."

Breathe.

Chapter Twenty-Five

Ghost

With my phone wedged between my shoulder and ear, my shoes slide on. Fire comes from every single pore. The guys are all piled in the truck. I step up, sliding into the passenger seat. Luke's leaning against the back seat, clearly waiting for an explanation. Cam leans his arms on his knees with wide eyes, waiting for the same thing. A scowl covers Ace's face while his hands tighten around the steering wheel. "Hospital. Now." I bark out. He throws it in reverse.

"Well, are you going to tell us what's happening?" Cam leans up even farther.

Attempting to gather my thoughts, my gaze meets each of theirs, "Something happened while Rain was at work. We'll find out more once we get there."

"Do you think it has anything to do with what's happening with us?" Cam chews on his lip.

"I'm not sure unless someone saw us when we went shopping or has been watching the house."

I should've stayed away. She's going to get hurt because of me, but I can't bring myself to regret a single thing.

We end up shaving ten minutes off the twenty-minute drive to the hospital. Ace skids to a stop in front of the glass entrance doors. Before the truck comes to a complete stop, I jump out, closely followed by Luke and Cam.

"Go ahead. I'll hurry," he yells at Luke and Cam.

The truck tires squealing fade as we step into the overpacked waiting room. My head swivels back and forth.

She's not out here. What if something happened while we were on our way?

My phone immediately meets my ear as my eyes dart around, continuing my search as I move down the hallway. Just as it goes to voicemail, a door slams open, and someone jumps into my arms.

Instinctively wrapping my arms around her, a sob breaks through.

Running my hand up and down her back to calm her, "I need you to breathe, baby girl. Breathe for me."

Sniffles sound from my shoulder. "I was terrified, Grey." Adjusting her in my arms only makes her cling tighter.

"I know, baby, but we're here. We'll figure it out."

My eyes meet Cam's. He manages to find an empty room at the end of the hall. Motioning inside, we all enter as he closes the door behind us. A hospital bed sits in the middle of the sterile white room with a curtain drawn halfway around it. The blanket is folded perfectly with the corners tucked. The temperature feels like it dropped ten degrees compared to the hallway. Walking over, taking a seat on the edge of the bed, I lean back attempting to peel Rain off of me just enough so I can see her.

"Sorry," mumbling as she leans back, refusing to look at any of us.

"Hey, don't be sorry. I need you to tell us exactly what happened, though, so we can figure out what's going on," Ace barges in, looking as concerned as we all feel.

She describes every detail from the time she rounded that corner. By the time she's finished, all four of us are shaking with rage. Anger has begun overtaking her as well.

Cam meets my eyes, "This will be the biggest mistake of that bitch's life. We'll figure this out."

Luke stomps out as his hand white knuckles his laptop, leaving to hunt down Ace's truck in the parking lot.

Cam runs out as the door slams behind him.

Ace's eyes land on Rain, "You okay?"

She nods, "I'd like to go to Cassi's." Her big eyes meet mine. " Can you stay with me for a little bit, please?"

"Of course, little bird," tucking a strand of hair behind her ear.

Setting her back down on the ground, we begin our way back outside, ensuring my grip on her hand never falters.

If something happened to her because of me.

Shaking my head, attempting to rid them of my mind. The corners of my mouth begin to turn up as I notice she's again holding her keys in the air, looking for her car. Thankfully, the parking lot has thinned compared to when we first arrived.

We pull up to Cassi's apartment. The sun hits down on the white building and perfectly kept shrubs. I couldn't bring myself to let go of Rain's hand on the ride over. Cassi runs out barefoot, wrapping her arms around Rain. Turning back to Ace, he avoids my eyes.

He called Cassi.

Looking over Rain's head, "Come on. Let's go inside."

We walk through the glass door and wait for the elevator to ding. Looking back at Ace, he looks extremely uncomfortable. We step in as the doors open. The silence is deafening. Stepping out, we follow Cassi to her door as she unlocks it.

"You guys can have a seat in the living room. Get whatever you need from the kitchen. We'll be upstairs."

Luke, Cam, and Ace all pile onto the light gray sectional buried under fluffy blankets. Walking over to Rain, I bend down and kiss her forehead.

"I'll be right here if you need me."

She gives a soft smile, "You better be."

SHADOWS AND DECEPTION

Chapter Twenty-Six
Ghost

As the door closes, "What the hell is going on?"

She stands with her hands on her hips, never moving her eyes from me. Dropping down on the bed and giving her the short version of what happened, her mouth drops.

"Look, I'm fine. I've calmed down. Am I shaken up? Absolutely. I'm tired of not standing up for myself. I'm done being that person, Cass."

"It's about damn time, Rain. I've known you since we were kids. You've never had it easy since your dad disappeared. This can't let this keep you from living your life. I'm not saying to dismiss it, but you can't live in a bubble of fear."

"I completely agree."

"We're going out. The Hideaway. Tonight."

Surprises cover my face. "You know they aren't going to let us out of their sight, much less go out to The Hideaway."

"Let me handle that, babe."

She walks over to her closet and throws the doors open. Shirts, dresses, skirts, and everything in between fly out as she slings them on the bed. She runs over with the crimson dress I bought.

"Where did you get my dress, and why didn't I notice before now?" a giggle escapes.

A mischievous grin spreads across her face, "You didn't want Ghost to see it before we had the chance to go out. I knew he would if you took it home, so I grabbed it and put it with mine. Now, put it on."

Stepping into the bathroom, my clothes drop into a pile on the floor. The dress slips over my head as the soft material slides down my body. Looking up in the mirror, my eyes rake over how it molds perfectly to my curves as the deep V-neck plunges down the front. At that moment, the bathroom door flies open.

"Oh. My. God! You look amazing, Rain! He will have a heart attack when he sees you in that. Sit down and let me work."

She manages to slide a chair into the bathroom. She pours her entire makeup bag onto the black vanity. She begins applying a light layer of foundation, a smokey eye, and a neutral lipstick. The curling iron meets my hair. Soft waves fall down my back. Turning around, it's my turn for my mouth to drop.

I feel beautiful.

Tears threaten to leak from my eyes, "Thank you, Cass."

"Don't you dare mess up your mascara. You look gorgeous."

"Your turn." A grin appears on my face.

She slips into her black dress and takes my place in the seat. Winged eyeliner comes to a point on her eyes, and deep red paints her lips. Sectioning her hair, the straightener slides down each strand, causing her midnight black hair to shine from the light.

A squeal leaves her lips as she looks in the mirror. "I love it! Thank you."

We slip on black heels. The nerves of going downstairs begin to creep in.

Her hand meets mine, "Put yourself first, Rain. Now, let's get this party going."

Before I can reply, she's grabbing my wrist and pulling me forward down the stairs. My nerves are replaced by the terror of falling and breaking my neck in these shoes. We round the corner. Ghost's eyes trail down my body as he gulps. Ace's reaction is the same for Cassi. A smirk plays at her lips as her hands meet her hips.

"Hot damn!" Cam pipes up as a boyish grin appears.

"Now, we're going out tonight-" Cassi begins.

"Absolutely not. Look at what happened today. Why the hell do you want to go out tonight of all nights?" Ghost snaps before anyone else can answer.

"Look at me, Ghost."

His eyes soften as they land on me. "You know my past. I refuse to let one more moment go by not living how I want to. You all are welcome to come with us, but like it or not, we're going. That woman could just as easily hunt me down at work again or even at the house."

He steps forward, placing his hands on either side of my face, "If something happens to you because of me, I could never forgive myself, little bird. Ever."

My lips meet his. Dropping my voice, "Then come with me."

Looking back as Ace's arms cross his chest, Luke sits back, watching the scene before him, and Cam bounces up and down on the edge of the couch.

"Fine."

A squeal leaves Cassi's mouth, pulling my attention away from the man before me.

"Thank you." Dragging him out the door, I toss a wink over my shoulder at Cassi, where she beams.

Everyone follows as we step onto the elevator. Ace, Luke, Cam, and Cassi pile into Ace's truck as Ghost and I decide to take my car.

As he opens the door and I slide into the seat, I feel his breath on my neck. Kisses trail up as his hand runs up my leg, pushing the hem of my dress up. His thumb gets closer and closer, slowly running over the thin layer of cotton.

Shaking my head, "Nope. You are not about to distract me. If you take me out right now, you'll have a surprise when we get home."

He groans as I lean forward, nipping at his lip.

Grinning, he nods, "Let's go then."

We're able to find a parking spot in the packed lot. The music blares through the air as the door opens and closes. Bickering gets my attention, followed by laughter. Focusing on the group ahead, my eyes land on Cassi and Ace going back and forth with each other as Luke and Cam break into laughter. Glancing up, Ghost's eyes meet. His head immediately snaps up as he returns to high alert.

Cassi notices us as she turns, "Thank goodness you're both here. These goons are driving me crazy."

Shaking my head, "Let's go get a booth and grab some drinks."

The scent of smoke fills my nose. People yelling over the music overwhelms my senses. Ghost wraps his arm around my waist as he senses the change in my demeanor. Ace steps closer to Cassi, but she's too busy taking in the scene before her to notice. Luke stays behind with his scowl still glued in place. Cam

is already over at the bar chatting up a woman who's clearly enjoying the attention.

Something's wrong.

The same feeling as before washes over me.

I'm being paranoid. Tonight's the night to relax and forget about everything that happened.

"Over here." My voice is barely audible over the noise, I lead everyone to an empty booth in the corner.

The server comes to take our orders.

"See, this is fun, isn't it?" Cassi's eyes light up.

"It is. Thank you for convincing me to do this."

She reaches over to squeeze my hand. Looking over, Luke, sitting on the outer side, is still as tense as when we first entered, followed by Ace, who is squeezed between the table and seat. Cassi sits beside me, leaning forward, taking her drink from the waiter. Ghost's arm lays possessively behind me as he sits on the edge of the booth. I'm unable to resist giggling at our situation.

Cassi and I are three drinks in. Our bodies have relaxed, and our minds start to clear from today's stress.

"We're going outside for just a second for some fresh air. We'll still be able to see you both through the windows. Is that okay with you?"

"Of course. Go ahead. We're just going to stay here anyway," a giggle leaves my lips. He kisses my head as he and the guys squeeze through the sea of people to the door.

"You guys are perfect for each other."

"I'm really happy, Cass. Truly happy," I pause, "What's going on with you and Ace-"

She cuts me off, "I've got to go to the bathroom. I'll be right back."

She bolts to the bathroom. I feel eyes burning into me. Looking up, to see Ghost smirking at me from outside. I blow him a kiss making his face morph into a smile. Cam blows one back, earning an elbow in the ribs from Ghost, which causes Luke and Ace to toss their heads back laughing.

That's the first time I've seen those men smile, but something else is wrong.

My head whips around, taking in every swaying body in the bar. A familiar pair of eyes meet mine from the hallway to the bathroom.

The eyes from the hospital.

I shove myself out of the booth, immediately running in that direction.

I have to get to Cassi.

My feet come to a halt at the entrance of the hallway, the door at the end slams shut. The woman is nowhere to be found. The light shines off of something on the floor. Reaching down with shaky hands, the necklace Cassi never takes off, glimmers in my hand. Bile rises in my throat. Turning left, I throw the bathroom door open. Every single stall door is empty; my hands grip my hair.

Nothing. She's not here. How could I be so stupid? We should've listened to them and stayed home.

SHADOWS AND DECEPTION

Chapter Twenty-Seven

Ghost

Turning around at the sound of feet running toward me, my hand instinctively grips my gun. The streetlamp finally gives in to the flickering as it burns out, leaving the street in a blanket of darkness. Ace is already on guard as terror pours over his face.

"Where's Cassi?" he strides toward the bar.

Taking her in as tears flow, my hands go to each side of her face. "Tell me what happened, baby."

"They-they took her," as a sob crashes through her.

Before she can get anything else out, Ace is bounding toward the door making it almost fly off the hinges. Rain drags behind me as we run to follow him.

Screams erupt through The Hideaway.

He turns with a deadly stare, "Which way?"

"Out the back, I think. She went to use the bathroom. We were about to leave."

Her hand grips mine in a death grip until my fingers tingle. We dodge people left and right as a beer bottle crashes in the back. Looking forward, Ace's shoulder meets the door, which slams open against the brick wall outside. The sound of a trunk closing grabs our attention. He takes off running as a large man jumps in, slamming the car door. Ace's fist connects to the window as the engine revs. The black car blends into the night as it takes off.

"No!" he roars.

"Get me the damn tag number!" Luke yells.

He turns as the taillights fade, connecting his fist to the brick. Blood begins trickling onto the pavement, barely visible by the moonlight. "Come on! We have to find her."

Taking off toward the truck, Luke slips into the front seat. He looks up with a smirk, "Get the fuck in. I've got them."

Ace rounds the truck and nearly tears the door off getting in.

I've never seen the man like this in any job we've been in. Ever.

"We'll be right behind you in Rain's car."

Following close behind Ace, we run every red light in the city. Luckily, not many people are out at this time. We take turn after turn, not slowing. Confusion takes over as we pass Rain's house.

A few blocks later, gravel flies up as we pull up to the house that's been under surveillance. Tonight was the one night nobody was watching- and they knew that. They must have.

"Everyone stay where they are. I'm going to look around first." Ace, barely able to contain himself, bolts out of his truck toward the house.

The sounds of crickets are the only thing keeping the silence away. I look over to find Rain has turned rigid. Her face morphs into complete panic, and her breathing becomes shallow.

Gripping her face on each side with both hands.

"What's going on? Come back to me."

Slowly blinking, moving her eyes to mine, "This is it."

"This is what?" rubbing my thumb over her cheek.

"This is the house I grew up in. The house my dad disappeared from. The house I was chained to for years because my mother refused to get herself help!" growing louder with each word.

Silence overtakes us until a sob escapes her, making her entire body shake with more force than I know what to do with.

"Look at me, Rain," moving her to face me, but she shrugs me off.

Her sobs continue to move throughout her entire body. Without thinking, I lean over, grabbing her by the waist, bringing her to straddle my lap with the soft glow of the light on the dash, enhancing her silhouette. Gripping the back of her head, I move it to my chest with my other arm circling her.

Slowly, her body relaxes as she sniffs. Leaning back, she seemingly looks into my soul. "Thank you," she whispers.

"I will chase away every thought that ever causes that reaction. Always. Do you understand?"

"You'll be doing a lot of chasing." The corners of her mouth turn up as she wipes her eyes.

Gripping the sides of her face again, letting her know every word I say is true, "Say you understand that, little bird. Please."

"I understand," she leans, pressing her lips to mine like she's pouring every emotion into me.

Pulling back, my hand runs through her hair. "I know this may not be the best time to say this, but I love you, Rain, with everything in me. On your good days and bad days, I love you." Her eyes light up.

As she opens her mouth to reply, one finger stops her lips from moving. "Don't say it right now. Once you say it, there's no going back. I need you to know that." She nods as her body melts into mine, her arms wrapping around my neck. "Do you want to go inside, or do you want to wait here? The choice is completely up to you."

She pauses and looks back to the house. "I'm coming with you. I need to face this."

Seeing Ace motion for us, "Let's go," opening the door and setting her down on the ground.

Instinctively pulling her closer, I wish I could protect her from whatever demons lay in wait for us. She looks up as my hand squeezes her side letting her know everything will be okay.

Nodding at Ace, Rain moves behind me. We move forward toward the door. Luke and Cam follow behind her. Moving around the house with our backs against the siding, we slowly step onto the porch, ensuring the boards don't creak. Each of us stays on either side of the door, listening. The sound of pots and pans filters their way outside from the kitchen window to the left of us. Glancing back, Rain's eyebrows crease in confusion.

Nobody should be in there.

The faint sound of a TV carries out as well. Nodding at him, his shoulder rams through the door, splintering the wood trim. As we move in, the TV and a single lamp missing the lampshade are the only light sources in what looks to be a living room- or used to be, anyway.

Behind us, Ace rushes through the room. "Cassi!" he bellows. He continues his search, breaking down doors. "Cassi, baby, answer me!" emotion overcomes him.

Sitting to the right of the initial room is a man with light exposing only half his face. Rain tenses behind me as she slowly peaks out behind me. Recognition sparks in her eyes, turning to unforgiving rage. Before anyone can catch her, she's walking toward him, shoulders held high, her fists clenching.

"Remember me?" she whispers.

The sound of a smack fills the room. My eyes widen, realizing the sound resulted from Rain's hand making contact with the man's plump face.

A look of shock paints his face as he leans up. She doesn't back down, still bent down in front of him. A hand stops me as my foot moves forward, glancing back to see Cam.

A maniacal grin takes over her face, "Hello, daddy dearest. Miss me?"

Ice-cold water pours down over my entire body.

163

Wait.

The man that disappeared from her life, the one who left her stuck in this hell hole, giving her no option but to care for the one who should've been caring for her? The one torturing women that are the same age as his own flesh and blood? That's the one sitting before us?

I return to the ongoing interaction, still attempting to process what's happening.

"You know I missed you, sweet girl." as he reaches for her. *He really is fucked up.*

Another smack rings out. Before any of us can move, he pounces, grabbing her by the neck and pinning her against the wall. She manages to laugh- she actually laughs in his face.

"I let that slide the first time, but not a second," he says as he raises his fist. I make it over in time to grip it, squeezing until the bones begin popping. He lets out a scream and drops to his knees as I start to twist his arm.

Nobody touches what's mine. Ever.

She looks down with a satisfied smirk, suddenly morphing into a mix of emotion.

Chapter Twenty-Eight
Rain

My father. The one that abandoned me. He's right here in front of me. He left me to believe he was dead or at least missing. For all these years, he's been right here. My emotions have become a storm. Ripped out of my thoughts, glass clinks against each other. My heart drops.

No.

Standing before me is none other than my mother, wearing a broad smile and holding a glass dish of lasagna like she's presenting a prized pig. She's not supposed to be here. She's not supposed to be out of that place. They didn't contact me- they don't if someone signs her out. My head jerks back to the man that Ghost has crumpled on the floor.

"You did this? You brought her here, and for what?"

He looks up, clearly in pain. "I love her. We could finally be happy without you. You were always in the way, constantly needing attention. We were exhausted by it. So, I supposedly dropped off the face of the planet as she pretended to be helpless. Ever wonder why her door was always closed?"

Blinking, unable to absorb what I just heard, "I was a child! Of course, I needed attention! You both were supposed to protect me, but you abandoned me! Do you know how hard it is for me to trust people now? How long I've been alone because of what you both did?" I screech.

Looking up at Ghost, his emotions are written clearly—disbelief accompanied by rage. Luke and Cam's faces show the same.

Remembering that the world's best mother is still standing in the doorway holding that stupid dish, sporting a smile. She clearly sees nothing wrong. I lean down to grip his hair to pull his head back. As soon as I do, a handful of my own hair is pulled back, making tears blur my vision. The cold metal meets my throat. Inhaling, the signature perfume that belongs to my mother, meets my nose.

"One move, and she's dead." she grinds out, causing a shiver to run down my body.

Clapping fills the air. "Do it."

Every head in the room snaps to the sound. Staring at me from the bottom of the stairs is the same pair of eyes from the bar. The same woman that threatened me with the knife in the hallway.

Why the hell is she here?

Glancing at Ghost, all the blood has drained from his face.

"Mom?" confusion is apparent in his voice.

"Hey, baby. Nice to see you again," she grins.

Luke and Cam are frozen with shock at everything that has just transpired.

Ace gets to a door that must be the basement. "It's locked!"

Unable to focus on that as the grip on my hair tightens.

Ghost's eyes jerk to me. I give him a slight nod or as much as my hair will allow. The blade presses harder against my skin.

"You're in on this? The drugging? The kidnapping?" Ghost's eyebrows draw together. Anger slowly pours over him as the shock wears off.

"Of course, honey. You left me a widow. I had to fill my schedule with something."

"He beat you! He beat Lily. I served myself on a silver platter. You made me into the monster I am! Don't you have any remorse for that?" disbelief evident.

"I loved him," she growls out as her mask slips.

"How? How did you get yourself into this mess?"

"After I walked out of that door, the day of your father's death, I checked myself in at Rosewood, where I met Rain's mother. I eventually met Ryan at one of his scheduled visits. My anger towards you and your sister paired with their anger toward

Rain helped us gain momentum to forge a plan. The whole drugging thing was just for fun. Those idiots who worked for us were useless. They even believed we had another man working with us. But, fast forward, and here you all are." She is seemingly proud of her work.

As my mother's attention is strictly held on the scene before us, Luke and Cam catch my attention as they face my direction. A scream escapes me as they dive directly into my mother's frame. My hand wedges between the blade and my neck, slicing my palm and causing blood to drip down my fingertips. They twist her arms behind her back. Ghost's mother looks on in horror, but it quickly disappears as Ghost drops my father into a heap on the floor and tackles her. A clatter is audible from her direction. Running, my hand wraps around it before she can move over and take it, knowing precisely what needs to be done. Turning, my gaze settles on my surprisingly calm father.

One step in front of the other.

Raising the gun, it points directly between his eyes.

"Where is she?" staring directly at him.

"Where's who?" with a smug look on his face.

"Tell me where Cassi is!" My hands shake as rage overtakes me.

His eyes quickly glance to the hallway to the left of the kitchen, but I catch the movement.

"Ace! She's not in the basement! Check the hallway," I yell out. Taking one step closer, the gun presses against his forehead.

He smirks, "I don't regret a thing."

"Stop!" I turn at the sound of Ghost's voice. "This will haunt you, Rain, for the rest of your life."

With a soft smile, "I'll sleep just fine. We all have a little bit of a monster inside of us."

Turning back around, the sound of a gunshot bounces off the walls. My mother's screams fill the air. Her body goes limp in their arms.

Nodding at Luke, "Call the cops. I want her put back in Rosewood."

Shock still flows through my veins. I looked down at my mother, wondering if she really meant what she said or if her sanity had finally snapped. I'm thinking the latter. Motioning for Luke to come over after he hung up to hold onto my mother- if you could even call her that. My eyes land on my father's lifeless body, surprising myself at the absence of emotion.

Ghost walks over. With one hand, he lifts my face to meet his. "Focus on me. It'll be okay, little bird."

Sniffing as my head buries into his chest. "Why was I too much? I didn't do anything wrong!" a sob comes out muffled.

"Shh, you're not too much. You are absolutely perfect.

I promise I'll make sure you're okay."

My eyes close as his lips meet my forehead, causing my entire body to relax.

Sirens blare, and red and blue lights shine through the window, lighting up the room and bringing us all back to reality.

An older man with salt and pepper hair makes his way up the front porch, slowly taking in the outside of the house. Cam reaches over to swing the door open.

He steps in, his eyes widening in shock.

"What the hell happened, Cam?" All of our heads whip around at the same time. "Well, hello to you too, Dad."

Oh shit.

He nods to each of us, "The name's Eric." We all stay silent letting everything sink in.

"The man on the floor over there kidnapped Cassi after checking his wife out of Rosewood, which she clearly still needs to be in. This one here in my arms is Ghost's mother, who I believe also needs a trip to Rosewood." He smiles proudly like he has just won a prize.

Shaking his head, Eric scans the room and comes to face me. "Is this true, young lady?"

My eyes shoot to Ghost, but Eric misses it. "Yes, sir, it is."

His eyes drill into me momentarily, "I'll take care of it."

My arms immediately wrap around him, "Thank you."

His hand awkwardly pats the top of my head and backs away. He heads toward the door but stops, pointing at Cam, "You and I are having a chat later."

Cam gulps, "Understandable."

Two men come in as Eric walks out the door. Their eyes almost bulge out of their heads. Attempting to be discrete but failing, they look at each other and shake their heads. Without a word, they place handcuffs on both women and lead them outside. A deep breath leaves all of us.

The sound of footsteps grabs our attention. The lamp lights up Ace's form as Cassi clings to his body. His arms are wrapped tightly around her. Her arms are wrapped around him as if she's afraid he'll disappear.

Ace's voice laced with emotion, "I'm going to take her to the hospital to get checked out."

"Of course. We'll follow behind you."

Cassi's head turns, "No, there's no need to. I'm perfectly fine. Ace will take me, and I'll call you when I get out. I promise."

Ace's face softens as he studies hers, wiping under her eyes. "I've got her, guys," he starts for the door.

"Be safe and call me as soon as you leave!" Rain calls out.

SHADOWS AND DECEPTION

Chapter Twenty-Nine

Rain

Ghost catches my eye, staring at me with a hint of a smile. Suddenly, a knowing feeling overcomes me.

Walking over, I stand in front of him, taking in all of his features. His eyes stand out the most. They've softened since we first met.

Running my hand up his chest, resting it on his cheek.

"Can I say it now?"

"Say what?"

"I love you too, Grey."

Our moment quickly ends as Eric pops his head back through the door, "You," pointing at Ghost, "come out here. I need you to tell me what happened for the report."

"Yes, sir."

Turning back, kissing the top of my head, "I'll be right back."

The feeling of someone behind me raises the hair on the back of my neck. My head snaps around to see Cam looking down at me.

Placing a hand on my shoulder, "Are you okay?"

My head begins spinning as the reality of what just happened hits me with full force.

Noticing my hesitation, he guides me to the back porch as the splinters of the wood almost scrape against my skin.

He sits down, patting the spot beside him.

Looking over, I notice the glow that usually lights up his face is replaced with a dark shadow. His eyes focus on me, but his past is clearly making a return.

Studying my face, "That's the first time you've shot anyone, isn't it?"

"Is it that obvious?"

Letting out a dark chuckle, "Yeah, Rain, it is."

He plucks an overgrown blade of grass sticking up on the side of the porch, staring at it like it's the most fascinating thing he's ever seen.

"I was 13," he whispers, taking a deep breath. "My parents got divorced soon after I was born. Dad was always on the job. He tried to do his best, but one day, my mom had enough. She took my two sisters and me across the country while he was at work," glancing up at the sky, "Growing up, we never had much. Our clothes always smelled of cigarette smoke, covered in dirt from mom not washing them. We were all bullied for it at school.

"Anyway, mom had random men in and out of the house, some worse than others. One night, I had trouble falling asleep. Something didn't feel right. I was watching a bug crawl across the ceiling when my sister's scream came from down the hall. Running as fast as I could, the piece of shit was on top of her, trying to cover her mouth. Mom had tried throwing a glass mug at her a few days before, but it shattered against the wall. I saw a shard of glass shining from the moonlight through the window. Without thinking, I grabbed it and jumped on his back. It kept driving into his neck as he gargled on his own blood. The sound still haunts me every single night. My clothes were soaked in blood. My sister was sobbing as she helped me push his body off of her. I didn't regret it though. I never have.

"Whether you know them or not, protecting someone is worth the nightmare. At least to me, it is. Anyway, the neighbors had heard the commotion and called the cops. Jumping out of the window was my only option to avoid getting caught. The bush below was tall enough to hide me. I listened to both of my sisters yelling as they were dragged out of the house. That's the night East found me, and I met the guys. I saw how haunted they were. There was a storm in all of their eyes. Deciding then, I refused to let that happen. But I have tried, since I first met them, to keep up a sunny persona so they wouldn't have to worry as much."

My hands cover my mouth as tears form in my eyes.

"Cam, I'm so sorry. I had no idea."

Shaking his head, "There's no need to apologize. They were protected. That's all that mattered."

"How did you get back to your dad?"

"Before East started using us for his dirty work, he helped me find where he was from what little information I had heard from Mom. It wasn't until I was older that I had enough courage to reconnect with him. He knows what happened that night and knows that I will continue doing it for the right reasons. For the people who can't protect themselves."

Wiping under my eyes, "Did you ever see your sisters again?"

His head drops, "No, but we both look for them daily. It's become an obsession at this point."

"How do you deal with what you've done? The nightmares. I figure they'll come at some point."

A sad smile falls on his face, "You learn to cope. You're lucky to have Ghost. He protects the ones he loves, unlike anyone I've ever met. Between you and me, he goes through the same thing. We all do. Just promise you'll let him help. Don't shut yourself off."

Nodding my head, "I promise. Thank you for telling me, Cam. You know you guys have been more of a family than I've ever had. I can't thank you enough."

"You've always got us. If things get to be too much, call any of us. Like I said, we've all been through it."

Luke and Ghost interrupt when they walk onto the porch. Ghost looks down as he walks up behind us, his brows drawn, "Is

176

everything okay?" Squatting down, running a hand over my hair, "Are you okay, little bird?"

A soft smile appears as I look between him and Cam, "I will be."

Cam claps his hands together as he shakes his head. His glow returns, "Can we leave, now? I'm hungry."

We all burst into laughter as the heavy atmosphere lightens.

Shaking my head, "Let's go."

SHADOWS AND DECEPTION

Chapter Thirty

Rain

The bell chimes as it brushes the top of the door as we walk into the diner. The place is almost empty, with only two tables occupied. The young waiter drags himself over to seat us. Dark circles are prominent under his eyes. Ghost motions for me to scoot in the booth first, causing the coolness of the leather to seep into the back of my legs. He slides in after me, followed by Cam and Luke sitting in front of us. Silence surrounds us after we each tell the poor boy our drink orders. Glancing out, a bird hops along the sidewalk causing a small smile to form.

"Well, that was interesting," Cam breaks the silence.

Luke scoffs, "You can say that again."

"Do you think Cassi's going to be okay?" concern laces Cam's voice.

Whipping around, "Of course she is. She's a firecracker, especially since Ace is staying there with her. She'll be fine."

I hope I'm right.

Ghost reaches over, wrapping an arm around my shoulders and gently tugs me into his side. The heat from his body begins to engulf me. Leaning up, I quickly kiss his cheek, drawing a smile from him as he looks down.

"You two are gross." Cam makes a fake gagging noise, causing us all to laugh as the tension eases.

I stick out my tongue at him as he jumps from the swift kick Ghost gives his leg under the table. Luke attempts to hide a smile while he shakes his head as Cam looks offended by Ghost and I. Laughter comes bubbling out, which gets the attention of the two couples sitting a few tables over. Giving a small wave of apology, my eyes land on Ghost, who is shooting daggers in their direction.

The waiter walks into his sight, thankfully bringing his attention back to the table.

"Is everyone ready to order?"

Everyone nods as we take turns explaining what we want. He hurries back to the counter, spitting out our order to the man in the kitchen. Smoke billows out of the tiny window, followed by a slew of curses.

Noticing how tense Ghost has become, nudging him in the ribs makes his head snap back around.

"Would you relax a little bit-" His phone dinging makes us all come to attention.

Attempting to study his expression with no luck, "Is it Ace? What did he say? Is Cassi okay-" his finger covers my lips.

"Little bird, hang on," he pauses as he continues reading, "Cassi is doing great. Ace said she's mostly shaken up, but he plans to stay at her place to look after her."

"That will be interesting," Luke mumbles.

Glaring at Luke, he continues, "They're leaving the hospital now, but he will have Cassi text you in the morning after she's gotten some rest."

A sigh of relief exits my mouth as the weight on my shoulders nearly disappears. Tears threaten to escape.

Ghost notices one as it runs down my face. He wipes it away before my body snuggles into his arm.

She's okay.

The atmosphere at the table lightens even more right before our food comes out. From burgers to chicken tenders, we all dig in. The adrenaline is finally wearing off as the hunger kicks in.

"So, is Cam going to spill the beans about his dad being the chief?" Luke comments.

Cam dramatically rolls his eyes, "He knows a little about what we used to do. We reconnected after we left East and agreed that no questions would be asked. He agreed since he knows we deal with pieces of shit like today. No offense."

"None taken. I'm not complaining, though," Ghost chimes in.

As the conversation continues, the waiter swings by to place the ticket on the table. Ghost, unsurprisingly, takes care of it.

Luke leans in, "If you ever need to talk about what happened, just let me know."

The warmth in my chest begins to grow, "Thank you. That means a lot."

Ghost strolls back to the table, holding a hand out. My hand meets his as he helps me scoot out of the booth. "Come on, little bird. Let's go home."

Home.

Squeezing his hand, I let him lead me out to the car. The car ride is quiet as we both process what happened earlier with our parents. Seeing my father sitting there poured a wave of emotions over me that I don't think I've even processed yet. I spent years thinking he had left us and years thinking that he was even dead. My mind turns to my mother standing there with that glass dish. I was exhausted for so long, and she didn't have a care in the world. But there's something worse,

I shot him. I shot my own father right between the eyes.

Bringing me out of my thoughts, "The first time is always the hardest, but in your case, it will be harder to accept," squeezing my hand, "but I've got you. I'm not going anywhere."

We pull up in front of the house—the moon light illuminates the walkway. Barking sounds from the inside as we rush to the door to unlock it. Snowball is sitting on the couch but soon runs up, jumping on my legs. Without hesitation, my arms scoop her up, peppering her with kisses. Turning around, Ghost stares at us, taking in the scene before him.

He snakes a hand around my waist, "Let's go to bed."

Walking across the room, Snowball lies in her bed, which is two sizes too big. Exhaustion hits us in full force on our way to the bedroom.

Peeling my shirt off, my shorts quickly follow. Ghost's eyes watch every movement like a lion watching its prey. Three steps later, I'm standing before him, pulling his shirt off his body. Smirking, it slips over his head. Shaking his head, he slips out of his pants and climbs into bed, patting the empty spot beside him. I walk over and place one leg over his lap.

Straddling him, my eyes take in his features, "Thank you," I whisper.

His eyebrows draw in confusion as he tucks a strand of hair behind my ear. "For what?"

"Loving me like I've never been loved before. Just thank you for everything."

"You don't have to thank me for doing something I don't even have to think twice about. I meant it when I said I'm not going anywhere," grasping my face with both hands, "You. Are. Mine."

Leaning down, I gently kiss his lips, suddenly needing him more than ever.

Leaning back, he looks into my eyes, "Trust me, I want this right now, but you're exhausted. You need to get some sleep first."

"Ugh, fine," flopping over onto the mattress.

He wraps a protective arm around me as a sense of peace overwhelms me.

My eyes begin to drift close as I hear, "I never thought this was possible."

"What wasn't possible?"

"Being genuinely happy and having everything I've ever wanted. It was always a dream that I forced myself to ignore. I'm the one that needs to thank you, Rain."

"I love you, Greyson."

"I love you too, little bird."

His words fade as sleep takes over.

The dimly lit room fills my vision, as does the man sitting in the corner. My father.

I left here earlier. No. I can't be back.

"Why'd you do this, Rain? What the fuck is wrong with you. My own daughter?"

"Stop. After what you did, I don't regret a single thing."

"But you will," a sadistic smile spreads across his face as a click fills the air. He raises the gun to me. He's not close enough for me to attempt to knock it out of his hands. My eyes screw shut to keep myself from seeing what's coming.

He laughs as the gun goes off. That's the last thing I hear as I open my eyes, realizing I'm still alive.

What the fuck?

Turning around, Ghost is lying in a pool of blood as his lifeless eyes drill into mine.

"No!" letting out a pained scream.

My father's laughter fills my ears as everything begins to shake.

SHADOWS AND DECEPTION

Chapter Thirty-One

Ghost

Rain's screaming pierces my ears, jolting me awake.

"Rain, baby, wake up!" grabbing her shoulders, attempting to wake her up.

Her eyes fly open. Her breathing returns to normal as she sees me hovering above her. Her hands find my shoulders. Taking her time, she moves from my shoulders up my neck and lands on either side of my face. She gently pulls me down, tenderly kissing my lips. My body shifts over hers, aware to keep my weight from crushing her. Her kisses grow frantic.

"Please," she breathes out, "Please, Grey. Make me forget."

"As you wish, tell me to stop at any time. Okay?"

Trailing kisses down her neck, her hands trail down my body, leaving my skin blazing. She grips me through my boxers, causing a gasp to escape.

"You're going to pay for that," I slow down, causing her to try and move herself against me to speed things up again.

The corners of her mouth turn up, "Beg."

My hand moves up, resting on her throat as I take her nipple in my mouth, sucking and teasing, "Please," I whisper.

Switching to the other side to do the same causes her to let out a cry as she arches her back, trying to get closer, "Please,"

I move down her stomach at a torturing pace.

"Forget begging. I need you. Right. Now," she moans.

"You've got me, always."

My fingers grip her thighs hard enough to leave bruises. Spreading her legs as wide as they will go, I dig in. My tongue licks up every drop that has leaked from her entrance. At a teasing pace, my tongue travels up her slit, causing her legs to tense. Smirking to myself, I swirl around her clit, licking and sucking. The soft skin glides across my tongue. As her legs begin to shake, I shove two fingers inside, causing her to scream as she climaxes. Once she rides it out, she props herself up on one elbow as she crooks a finger at me, motioning for me to come up.

Moving up until my body is flush against hers, she grabs the back of my neck, meeting my lips. Never breaking the connection, she slides my boxers down as far as she can, giggling when she realizes she's not making much progress. With a chuckle, I slip them the rest of the way off as she grabs my cock without warning.

With one touch, she sets me on fire. My length glides back and forth, her wetness coats it as she begins moving her hips. I pull back, making her gasp.

"Flip over. Now."

She does as she's told, which puts her pussy on perfect display when she backs up on her knees. My eyes burn the image into my mind. My hands meet her ass, making her let out a cry.

She turns back with a mischievous grin. "Harder."

I can do that.

My hand comes down with more force on the other side. Shoving myself inside her before she has any time to respond, she grips the sheets as she lets out a moan that makes me even harder.

"You're going to take every inch like a good girl, aren't you?

She turns her head to look back as she bites her lip and nods. Slamming back into her, her head falls, bracing herself, knowing it won't be ending anytime soon. Her moans continue filling the room.

Reaching forward, my fingers enter on each side of her mouth, "That's it. You're being such a good girl."

With each thrust, the urge to let go grows, "Do you want me to make you cum now, little bird?"

One hand slips to wrap around her throat while the other travels down the front of her body, circling her clit. Her head leans back against my shoulder. Her hands come up to grip my hair— her body tenses.

At that moment, her entire body convulses. As she rides it out, I continue pounding into her until my cum fills her up. Pulling out, we both attempt to catch our breath. The walk to the bathroom is short as I return to see that she's still sprawled out on the bed, causing me to chuckle.

"You killed me. Completely killed me." She mumbles into the blanket, still refusing to move.

"I'm not sorry. Not one bit," leaning down, still chuckling as the warm cloth cleans her.

Looking up, those chocolate eyes stare back at me, "I never thought it could be possible either," she whispers.

"What do you mean?"

"What you said earlier. Being happy. I didn't think it was in the cards for me until I met you,"

"I promise I'll spend every day for the rest of my life proving to you that it is,"

My arms scoop her up and gently lay her down, covering her with the blanket. It takes no time for her to turn, making her way onto my chest.

"So will I."

The feeling of something around my throat makes me jolt awake. Looking down to see Rain still asleep, my hand moves to my neck. Realizing over half of her hair is draped over my face and in my mouth, my muscles relax. The corners of my mouth turn up, and my hand gently brushes the hair away.

A giggle erupts from beside me.

"Sorry." She blinks as she adjusts to the light.

Shaking my head, "Come on. You need food."

"No," she pouts, "I want to stay here. In this bed. With you."

Laughter escapes as she sticks her lip out attempting to hide a smile.

"You were such a good girl last night. What happened?" dramatically shaking my head.

Swinging my legs over the edge, sneaking a peek at her, she lays there with her mouth open at what I just said.

"You did not-"

"Oh yes, I did go there."

Before she can say anything else, my shorts slide up my legs as I walk out the door.

SHADOWS AND DECEPTION

Chapter Thirty-Two

Rain

Unable to keep from laughing, my body flops back onto the bed.

Staring at the ceiling, the thoughts of everything that's happened over the past 24 hours hit me.

That nightmare last night.

I never knew true terror before now. Feeling nothing now about putting a bullet between my own father's eyes, the realization hits that I would rather rip my own heart out than lose Ghost. My heart begins to race, sweat pools on my skin, panic crashes into me in waves.

Calm down. Just breathe.

With a deep breath, my breathing manages to return to somewhat normal. My eyes land on his shirt lying in the corner, begging to be worn. His scent wraps around me as it slips over my head, instantly calming my racing mind. My head pops around the corner to see Ghost without a shirt, wearing one of my tiny aprons that was probably collecting dust in some drawer.

"You better finish admiring me before our food gets cold," his head snaps around, catching me in the act.

"I'll have to schedule it again at another time then. Thank you for making breakfast. It smells amazing,"

"You're welcome," walking past me, he leans down to kiss my forehead as he sets two plates on the table.

Breaking the silence, "Do you have anything planned today?"

"I need to meet up with the guys at some point. Luke texted me earlier with another job," his eyes never meeting mine.

"Hey, what's wrong?" tipping his chin up with my finger, forcing him to meet my eyes.

Gulping, "I was wanting to talk to you about something,"

Dread washes over me, "Okay, let's hear it."

"Well," he draws out.

"Would you spit it out? You're killing me."

"Fine. I was wondering if you wanted to move in together. Officially. Here or at my place, it doesn't matter. I can't handle the thought of not sleeping beside you every night or not being able to come home to you."

Processing everything he just said, "Well, duh. We haven't been apart since you got that stupid bullet in your leg. You can't get rid of me now if you tried."

Standing up, breakfast forgotten, he presses his lips against mine as he pours every emotion into it. Reluctantly, he eases back down in his seat. Unable to hide the pout that forms on my face, his grin grows even larger.

"You know, since we've always stayed here, I'm not sure I've even been to your house. Is that terrible?" a giggle escapes.

"Eh, probably. Lily's probably raided it since she knows where the key is now. We can go by today to see what you think."

"I would love that. Would it not bother you, though? The inevitable flowers that will be planted are nonnegotiable," shrugging my shoulders.

"If you want to paint the damn house pink, go ahead. As long as you're with me, do whatever you want."

"I think you're going soft, Grey,"

"Only for you." he returns to shoveling waffles into his mouth.

SHADOWS AND DECEPTION

Chapter Thirty-Three
Ghost

She said yes. Oh. My. God. She said yes.

I've grown to know what happiness is since she entered my life, but this feeling is something else. Something beyond happiness. Maybe she's right. Perhaps I am going soft. But I'm perfectly okay with that.

Finishing breakfast, I see her trying and failing, to discreetly give Snowball a small piece of bacon.

"I knew it! That's why she's been stuck to your side," attempting to glare at her.

She throws her head back, laughing, "It most certainly is not. How dare you imply that. I'm an enjoyable person to be around, and that's all."

Dramatically rolling my eyes, I pick up our empty plates and load them into the dishwasher.

"Come on. Let's see what you think of my place."

"Okay, hang on."

She hops down and goes to the bedroom. She returns wearing a pair of shorts and sandals, still looking like a goddess. Sneaking past her to grab another shirt since she decided to steal mine, I smack her on the ass, causing her to squeal. Hearing laughter, even after walking away, makes me smile.

Slipping on my shirt, "Come on, slowpoke! I'm ready!"

"Would you hold on a second? I'm coming."

"No, that's what you were doing last night," she mumbles.

"I heard that."

Giggling as she walks out the door, she's waiting by her door.

She plops in the seat, wiggling her legs excitedly.

The ride over involves more finger drumming, head banging, and out-of-key singing.

Pulling into the driveway, she gasps, "This is beautiful, Greyson!"

Her eyes widen as she takes everything in. It's dark and cold compared to hers. I'm not sure how that reaction came to be. She doesn't even wait for me to get out of the car. She's vibrating with anticipation as she waits for me on the porch. The door creaks open, exposing the dark entryway. It opens up with the living room to the right. The large window lets the natural light shine through.

Walking over, she looks out, studying the view, "This is amazing, Grey. I couldn't even see this from the driveway."

She walks over, running her hand over the brick fireplace. The rough texture rubs against her soft skin. She looks around, her eyebrows draw together. She walks back to the entryway, studying the stairs, but continues past. She continues into the dining room, where the dark oak table sits. It's been collecting dust for years. No one besides Lily has been in here. The room connects to the kitchen on the other side. She steps in, taking in the black cabinets and wooden countertop. The view above the sink, looking out into the backyard, draws her attention. The wooden swing hangs from the weeping willow tree next to a small pond surrounded by overgrown weeds I've been neglecting. She hasn't made a peep since she's been taking herself on a tour, making me unusually anxious.

Why do I want her to like it so much? Maybe it's because it's an extension of myself?

She turns and walks back to the stairs.

Motioning upward, "Can I?"

"Of course."

She begins stepping carefully up the stairs, taking in every detail of the handrail. Another large window viewing the backyard takes up most of the wall. She pauses to study everything as she has been.

At the top of the stairs is a hallway to the left leading to two rooms, one of which is my bedroom, or what used to be anyway. The hallway on the right leads to two more rooms that I never decided what to do. One bedroom in each hallway looks over the front yard, while the two others overlook the backyard.

She makes her way, entering each room. She examines the bedroom as her eyebrows draw together again as she takes everything in, which only increases the anxiety that's growing.

I've never been nervous before. Ever.

She spends a little extra time entering the room in the other hallway.

Noted.

Softly closing the door, she begins her descent down the stairs. Stepping onto the front porch, she turns, meeting my eyes.

"Here."

"What?" confusion is now taking over.

"I want this to be our home," a large grin takes over, "I'm absolutely in love with it."

A wave of relief washes over me, "Why did you have that look in the living room and bedroom?"

"It's cold. You don't have any touch of you other than the details most people may miss, but no pictures. Why?"

"I've always kept things simple. I haven't allowed myself to get close enough to people to have pictures hanging on every wall."

"I can understand that, but if you are okay with it, I choose here."

Wrapping my arms around her waist, "Whatever you want. I'll give you the world if you ask."

She grabs my shirt, pulling me down as she raises on her tiptoes. Pressing as close as possible, her lips meet mine.

Reluctantly peeling myself away, "Come on. Let's go." "And where are we going?" she looks up at me.

"It's a surprise and we're taking my car since I finally came back here," taking her hand.

The shiny black paint reflects as the garage door opens.

She missed noticing it when we first arrived.

The leather seats meet her skin as she sits down. Sliding in the seat molds around me. My fingers tighten around the steering wheel.

I can finally stretch my legs out.

Backing out, the garage door closes once we clear the door. Glancing over as we drive down the busy road, Rain has her hand out the window with her head back, eyes closed, and a hint of a smile on her face.

Our reflection bounces off the side of the buildings as we pass. Taking a side road, we pull up in front of the old brick building that is tucked away, still sticking out compared to the larger modern buildings around it. She studies its appearance quickly, noticing the glowing sign barely visible through the window. *Toasty Treats Bakery.*

A giant grin spreads across her face once she realizes where we are.

Rubbing the back of my neck, "I know you have a sweet tooth, so I thought you might like this place,"

"Are you trying to make this the best day ever because you are succeeding."

She doesn't even wait as she starts for the door. The bell chimes as we enter. An older woman with an apron covered in every icing color appears from around the corner. The place is small but somehow still cozy. The light pink paint coats the walls as pictures of different sweets hang above the tables.

"Welcome to Toasty Treats Bakery. What can I get for y'all?"

Rain steps up, examining everything through the glass case.

"What's your favorite?"

"I'm a sucker for chocolate. Here you go. Try this," reaching her what's labeled a chocolate fudge brownie.

Her eyes light up as she takes a bite. "Oh my goodness," she hits my chest, getting my attention, which hasn't left her since we came in. "This is absolute heaven. We'll take four!"

Shaking my head, the corners of my mouth turn up as I reach the lady my card. Rain's almost jumping up and down with excitement. She drags me to a table when the brownies meet her hand.

"Here. You have to try this. Two for me and two for you."

Taking a bite, I now understand her reaction.

This really is heaven.

Crumbs fall in front of her as she inhales the first one. Already deciding only to eat one, I reach her the second.

"Thank you," she whispers.

202

"You're welcome, angel. I love seeing you like this."

She beams as she licks her fingers after she devours the second one.

As I look out the window, thoughts begin swirling in my head, "You really would rather move into my place? I don't want you to feel obligated to."

"Grey, I want to share that place with you. There's no question about that," a soft smile appears.

"When would you want to?"

"This weekend," looking down, "I'm excited. Sorry if that's too soon."

Tipping her chin up, "That's perfect."

As expected, she finishes the third brownie happily.

As we head out the door, the bell chimes as she yells back, "Bye, Loretta! We'll see you later."

"Bye!"

Chuckling, "How did you know her name?"

"Name tag. Plus, she's precious. I hope you know you started something. This is becoming a regular thing."

"Anything for you," I whisper.

As we go back home, I pull my phone out dialing Cam. "Hey, man. Long time no see."

Rolling my eyes, "We just saw each other the other day. I need your help with something this weekend if you're free."

"Okay, shoot."

"Can you help Rain and I move into my place?"

A long whistle sounds on the other end, "It's about time you both made it official. Of course, I'll help. I'll let Luke know. Ace has been MIA since he's been at Cassi's, so it may just be us."

"That's fine. Thank you. I owe you." "Anytime." The call ends.

Looking over at Rain, she's already staring back, "So we can?"

"Yes, little bird. We can."

She lets out a squeal as we pull into the driveway, "I have some boxes we can use to get most of it packed up."

She's inside, digging through her closet before I can respond.

Spending the next few hours packing as much as we can, we're exhausted afterward. Our movie nights have continued even through everything we've dealt with, which has surprised me. Looking over, taking her in as she sleeps, I can't help but think back to the first time my eyes opened in the hospital and saw her face.

Who knew it would lead us here?

My hands cradle her feet as I stand, setting them back in my seat. Leaning down to her ear, "I'll be back in a little bit, little bird."

She doesn't flinch. My feet dive into the old black boots before they carry me to my car.

Chapter Thirty-Four
Rain

Best. Day. Ever.

Warmth covers my body as my eyes open with his arms wrapped around me. I've never been good at making friends or trusting people after what happened with my parents, but he's somehow managed to tear down my walls brick by brick.

He's been carrying me to bed every night after falling asleep on the couch. His hand moves through my hair as his heat seeps into my skin. Turning my head, pressing a kiss to his palm, he gives me a soft smile, looking at me with so much love that it's almost overwhelming.

"Today's the day," he whispers.

The last couple of days have flown by. The living room is buried underneath mountains of boxes.

"Get up, you two!" Cam yells from the hallway.

Our eyes widen, "How the hell did he get in?" I whisper-yell at him.

"I have no idea, but we're getting another lock on the new door."

Slipping on his shirt and jeans, he walks out the bedroom door. Opening it just enough to squeeze through so Cam can't see inside.

"What the fuck, Cam?"

"Come on, grab a box and let's start loading everything up."

Hearing Luke grumble makes me giggle. Swinging my legs over the bed, the coolness of the morning air hits my skin. Opening my closet door, only one outfit is still left hanging. Slipping it on with the sandals by the door, I pack away the last of the sheets.

Music begins blaring from Cam's phone as they continue to load boxes up and start grabbing the furniture. Standing in the bare living room, unable to keep myself from taking everything in.

I came here to escape my past. To get away from what I went through. I'm finally ready to start on my future. The one I created. The one I'm going to happily enjoy with the man I love.

Speaking of which, arms wrap around my waist as his head rests on my shoulder.

"You ready?"

"I've been ready since the moment you asked."

Chuckling, he grabs Snowball leaving the door open for me. With one last look around, the door latches.

On the way over, Snowball managed to wiggle out of Ghost's grip to shuffle over to me. Pulling up, the enormous oak trees greet us. Realizing just how much Ghost has opened up over the past year, this place no longer suits him. It's closed off and cold. Excitement runs through me at the idea of changing it from a house to a home.

Our home.

Holding Snowball in one arm, my phone begins ringing from my back pocket. Cassi's name lights up the screen.

"Cassi! Are you okay? How have you been-"

A giggle escapes her, "Slow down, Rain. I'm feeling a lot better. I'm sorry I haven't seen you lately."

"You've needed time for yourself, which is completely understandable. You know I'm here when you're ready,"

"Speaking of which, what's going on with Ace? He's been quiet-"

"Ghost has changed you," changing the subject. "In a good way," she adds.

Rolling my eyes, knowing exactly what she's doing, "We're moving in today. You guys will have to come see it once we finish up."

"I'd love that. I'll let you go, though. Call me later. I love you, Rain," she pauses, "and thank you for coming after me."

"You would do the same for me, Cass. I love you, too." The call ends as grumbling to my right meets my ears.

"You're all moved in. Please do something with this place. It's dark and dreary. It needs some sunshine." He mumbles as he walks away.

That it does.

Walking inside, I'm instantly lifted into the air.

"Wait, I have something to show you."

His hand grips mine as he leads us upstairs as confusion paints my face.

"What are we doing?"

He doesn't utter a peep, but opens the door to the room in the right hallway. It's the same one I was drawn to the first time I saw it. My eyes roam over every detail as my hands cover my mouth.

"Grey," I whisper. His hands are clasped behind his back as he looks around avoiding eye contact.

"I saw your paintings- the ones that made you cry. I saw how your face lit up when you began painting me. I thought now you could have a room to create ones that make you happy. I never want to see you cry again, little bird. It rips my heart out every time."

Canvases of all sizes line the walls, every color of paint lies on the table in the corner perfectly organized, and the easel sits directly beside the large window looking over the backyard. A small stool is pulled up in front of it with a tray of paintbrushes to the right.

My eyes meet his, "I'm speechless, Grey. This is beyond amazing. I'm not sure I can even thank you enough for this."

"You don't have to thank me. I only want you to be happy."

Moving in front of him, my lips meet his to express how thankful I am.

He did this for me.

SHADOWS AND DECEPTION

Chapter Thirty-Five

Ghost

"We're done. We'll see you later. Let us know if you need anything," Cam yells from the backdoor as it closes.

The soft kiss turns frantic. Unable to get enough, my hands travel down her body, lifting her shirt. Her hands grip the hem of mine as she desperately tries to take it off. Walking her back, she hits the door. In one swift motion, her legs are around my waist. Pressing my hard length into her, showing her what she does to me, causes her to let out a moan. Ripping her bra off that lands somewhere across the room, my fingers dig into her thigh as my other hand grips her wrists, pinning them above her head. My eyes take in the sight before me. With the tiny bit of self-control that remains, my lips start at her jaw, biting and sucking their way down. Giving her a small amount of relief, my mouth connects with her nipple. Swirling my tongue around, she moans as her hips begin to move against me. Biting down hard, giving her a mix of pleasure and pain, she looks down, meeting my eyes as my mouth moves to the other side.

Gently setting her down, "Take them off. Now," a demanding tone laces my voice.

Her entire body is on display, making my mouth water. In one swift motion, my hand grips a handful of her hair as a smile appears on her lips. Guiding her back, she stops in front of the table.

She leans back on her hands as she slowly opens her legs showing just how soaked she's been. Lifting her ankle, the torturous pace begins with kisses up her leg backing away before she has me where she wants. Lifting the other, the teasing continues. She gasps as my tongue runs along her slit. With her hands gripping my hair, the licking continues as she throws her head back. Without notice, my tongue dives in as her legs widen.

"Yes, just like that, Grey."

Her legs begin shaking, but before she can cum, two of my fingers plunge in, pumping in and out, causing her to explode. Shoving my pants and boxers down, my fingers are around her thighs, dragging her to the edge, "Have you been my good girl?"

"Yes, I've been good for you. I promise."

"You're going to take as much as I tell you, aren't you?"

Leaning in to bite her lip, my cock runs over her slit.

Bringing her head forward, "Watch."

Her eyes are glued to me as she watches me slam into her. Her eyes screw shut for a moment, but once they open again, they never leave where we're connected. My hands travel up, pinching each nipple, followed by wrapping my hands around her throat to keep her in place. The bouncing continues as she looks at me with a mischievous grin. Moving one hand back down, my thumb circles her clit. She closes her eyes, letting out a scream as her orgasm runs through her. My hands grab her hips, and in one swift motion, she's flipped over against the smooth wood.

Barely able to growl out, "You're not done."

Slamming into her once more, her breath grows heavy. My fingers move up until they enter her mouth. My hips move faster and harder. Knowing I won't last much longer, my free hand moves around circling her clit. Again, her legs begin to shake as she lets out a moan. Right before her legs give out, my cum fills her up. Slowly moving back, my eyes are unable to move from the sight of it dripping out of her sweet pussy.

Deciding to worry about our clothes later, my arms wrap around her as I lift her. Her eyes stay closed the entire walk to the bedroom earning a chuckle. She refuses to let go as we slide into bed.

She lets out a yawn. Sleep overtakes both of us.

SHADOWS AND DECEPTION

Chapter Thirty-Six

Rain

The house is spotless after months of procrastinating because there was always one single box that needed to be unpacked.

Why did nobody tell me? Is that normal?

Hearing his steps as the front door closes, he walks by the doorway with his nose in his phone.

Clearing my throat, "You forgot something."

He backs up as his head snaps to me, "Trust me, I didn't forget." He walks toward me and wraps his arms around my waist.

"Did you not see the surprise?"

His brows draw together in confusion, "What surprise?"

"You're kidding," placing my hands on my hips and raising a brow.

"You know you look beautiful today as always."

"No, don't even try that," the corners of my mouth turn up.

Grabbing his hand, he follows. Stepping onto the front porch, his mouth drops.

"How the hell did you manage this?" taking in the fact the oak trees have been cut down and replaced with dogwood trees.

No more hiding.

"It's perfect," bringing me in for a kiss.
Ringing peels us away from the little bubble that we've created.

A frown appears on my face. With no greeting, "Where are you?" my manager, Debbie, barks out.

"I'm off today," an edge in my voice that hadn't been present before. My feet begin carrying me back and forth on the porch. Glancing over, Ghost is texting away.

"Don't use that tone with me. Get in here. Someone called in," ending the call without waiting for a response.

Turning to see Ghost studying me with a softness in his eyes, "I have to go to work for a little bit. I'm sorry."

The corners of his lips turn up before he quickly returns to the previous expression he was wearing.

"That's fine. No reason to be sorry. I have to meet up with Luke and Cam anyway, so it works out."

He locks the door and begins his way down the steps. Reaching out and grabbing his hand, we walk back to the car.

"Go ahead and take your car to work. I think it's about time I take my car for a spin," he smirks.

"Fine, but don't think for one second that this gets you out of being my personal chauffeur."

He laughs, "I would never. For your information, I happen to enjoy it."

He opens the driver-side door. As I sit down, he leans in for one more quick kiss.

"Be safe. I love you," yelling across to him while backing out.

A smile takes over, "I love you, little bird," dramatically clutching his chest with one hand while reaching out the other.

Rolling my eyes, my blood pressure rises as the thoughts about going to work pour in. Thankfully, the extra scrubs in my trunk keep me from having to go back inside.

Unfortunately, having to park at the very back due to the overpacked parking lot, makes the walk inside feel like an eternity.

The lobby is filled to the brim with patients. A woman is rocking back and forth as she grips her hair, almost pulling it out. The woman beside her has her nose held high as she taps her sky-high stilettos on the plain white tile. The annoyance from her is palpable.

Deep breath, Rain. Deep breath.

The beep of the time clock, once again, pierces my eardrums. One step out of the small room, and the chaos begins. One room in particular catches my eye. Multiple nurses bolt in as white coats even flash by. My attention is on high alert while jogging after them. Shoving my way through, freezing as everyone attempts to back out discreetly. I notice Luke and Cam back out of the room as well with smiles on their faces. Even Debbie is smiling as she walks out. But then-

Eyes the color of ice meet mine. The same eyes I wake up to every morning. The steel blue eyes I'm in love with. The same eyes I knew I had to have when I saw him in this exact room.

"Hey, what are you up to?" a smirk plays on his lips.

Confusion swirls through my mind, "Hey? Are you okay? Are you hurt?" instantly moving close enough to inspect him.

"I'm in one piece, so don't worry. I needed to talk to you about something,"

"You caused absolute anarchy just to talk to me? I was just with you Grey," hands on my hips.

His hands replace mine, "That night at The Hideaway, I knew I wanted you, but in this room, I knew I needed you. As dramatic as it sounds, even death couldn't keep me from that fact. Over the past year, you've somehow brought me out of the shadows. You've helped me deal with the demons that I've suppressed my entire life. I love you, Rain, with everything in me. I want all of you. Forever. I need you. Forever. So,"

Tears are already filling my eyes as he slips off the table.

"Will you marry me, little bird?"

"Of course I will, Grey!"

His arms are instantly around me as he swings me around in the air. Setting me down, his hands grip my hair as his lips crash into mine. Pulling back, unable to keep myself from beaming with overwhelming happiness, my pinky rises in front of his face.

A grin spreads across his face as his finger meets mine, "Pinky promise."

"Pinky promise."

Taking my hand, he leads us out of the room, where more cheers and whistles erupt—looking over to see Luke smiling as Cam jumps up and down with a thumbs up. Nudging Ghost to look at them, we both burst into laughter. Debbie catches my eye wearing a smile that is undoubtedly foreign to her face.

Smirking as she approaches, "Does this mean I don't have to work today?"

"I'm sure he would have a problem with it if I said yes," nodding at Ghost.

"Thank you, Deb. Keep that smile. It looks good on you," turning to walk away.

"Go enjoy your fiancé before I change my mind!"

A giggle escapes as he leads me through the glass double doors, starting the mile hike back to wherever my car is parked.

A chuckle sounds from beside me, "You really do that every time, don't you?"

"Don't act surprised. You knew this from day one."

My keys stay in the air until the faint beeping becomes closer. My car comes into view as Ghost walks ahead to open the door.

Sliding in, he says, "Thank you for making me the happiest man in the world. I have to swing by Cam's for a second, but I'll meet you at home."

"Be safe. I love you, Grey."

His smile grows as he leans down and kisses my forehead, "I love you, too."

He disappears from my rear-view mirror as the nerves begin to grow.

This is it.

Chapter Thirty-Seven

Ghost

My eyes squint, attempting to keep the light out of my eyes as the sun begins to set. Cam and Luke's laughter fills my ears as my car comes into view.

"What the hell are you two doing?"

Luke claps his hand on my shoulder and grins, "We just wanted to come tell you congratulations."

Cam pipes up, "Don't bother coming over this evening."

Raising an eyebrow at Luke and his unnatural smile, "What's wrong with you two?"

"Nothing. Now, it's time for you to celebrate. We'll see you later," pushing me closer to my car.

Rolling my eyes, they turn, walking away before anything can come out. The leather molds against my body as my fingers grip the steering wheel. Unable to contain the excitement still flowing through me, my foot presses the pedal to the floor. Shaving off ten minutes, the car slides into the driveway.

It's empty.

One single lamp from the living room is the only light source visible in the house.

Rushing through the gate, "Rain?"

Silence fills the air. My lungs begin to burn as my legs carry me from room to room as panic pours over me. No other lights are on. Taking two steps at a time, "Rain?"

With every room empty, my feet slow as they near our bedroom door.

She has to be in here. What if something happened to her on her way home?

The door creaks open. The sunset causes the room to glow. My eyes land on a piece of paper lying on the bed.

Meet me in the shadows.
-Little bird

The panic lessens, but discomfort is still present in my chest, knowing it won't leave until she's standing in front of me. After pacing a hole in the floor, it finally clicks.

Taking the stairs as fast as possible, my life flashes before my eyes as the last step seems to disappear. Thankfully, my reflexes are fast enough to keep me from landing on my face. Gripping the doorknob, the door swings open, causing it to bounce off the wall. My lungs burn as the car door opens. The birds take off from the trees as the tires squeal.

Each light is somehow green as The Hideaway comes into view. Throwing the car in park, my eyes scan the area. The steady glow of the light on the pavement makes me notice the streetlamp isn't flickering anymore.

Someone finally fixed it.

My eyes snap to that familiar alley. Leaning against the same brick wall from what feels like so long ago is a silhouette that's become ingrained in my mind. The evening sun bounces off the brick wall.

Throwing the car in park, my steps echo beneath me in the remaining light of the day.

Standing in front of her, my eyes study her up and down. Interrupting my thoughts, she begins, "Notice anything?"

I study her further, "No. What am I missing?"

Rolling her eyes, "You're not very observant. Look up."

My eyes widen in shock. Stepping back, The outline of a couple standing closely together against a soft, glowing light is painted across the brick taking up most of the wall. Although their faces are lost in a shadow, their posture tells the story clearly.

Looking down at her as she chews her lip, "We've created our own life, our own story. Two people that emerged from the shadows and stepped into the light together," she pauses, "it's amazing to be able to experience what we both believed was impossible. I love you, Grey-"

My arms wrap around her before she can finish as I swing her around in the air making her squeal. The sound of cheers, clapping, and whistles interrupt the silence. Looking over to see Luke and Cam walking out of The Hideaway, grins cover their faces as they continue their celebration.

"You knew she did this?" yelling across the street.

Cam crosses the street and explains, "She asked us to keep you distracted long enough so she could run home. Thanks to Luke's face, your confusion allowed her just enough time. We didn't know that she did this, though." He looks up to study the image nodding in approval.

Luke interrupts, "I may have kept her company so she wasn't alone out here."

Meeting his eyes, with sincerity I say, "Thank you."

Cam suddenly turn serious, which grabs my attention, "You're not like yours. Remember that."

Without waiting, he turns to walk back to the truck with Luke—his words bouncing around in my head.

"He's right, you know."

Looking down, "And you won't be like your parents. We've both seen what not to do. Thank you for giving me what I thought was only a dream."

She stands on her tiptoes as she gently presses her lips against mine.

Unable to wipe the smile from my face once she pulls back, "Let's go home."

She goes to pull away when my hand grabs hers, "And where do you think you're going?"

Rolling her eyes, "I have to drive home."

"No," scooping her up in both arms, she doesn't bother protesting as her arms automatically wrap around my neck.

Gently setting her down in the seat, a sigh escapes her lips, "I'm happy, Grey. Genuinely happy."

"Me too, little bird."

Pulling into the driveway, I smile as my eyes land on her sleeping form. She doesn't stir when her head meets my chest as my arms wrap around her once again. Freezing as the porch creaks, and as usual, she still doesn't move.

SHADOWS AND DECEPTION

Chapter Thirty-Eight

Rain

"Greyson!"

The door swings open with him wide-eyed, "Are you okay? I thought I saw you sniffle earlier?" He places the back of his hand on my forehead.

Swatting it away, rolling my eyes, "Would you stop that? I'm perfectly fine. I tried calling Cassi to tell her about everything that happened yesterday, but she didn't answer any of my calls. She always answers. I don't think I've ever heard her voicemail. What if something's wrong?"

Tilting my head up, "Let's go over there just to make sure she's okay. With everything that happened, let's double-check. Will that make you feel better?"

Biting on my lower lip, I nod as my thoughts swirl. He's out the door as my mouth opens. Shaking my head at the sound of him almost tripping down the stairs.

Placing the brushes in the glass cup, the colors of the paint swirl in the water. The canvas before me isn't like what it used to be. No more tears flow like they did before. The wooden swing hanging from the tree in the backyard catches my attention as it moves gently in the wind.

He picked this room for a reason.

As the stairs come into view, Ghost stands by the door. A chuckle escapes as the cool wood touches my feet.

Slipping on my sandals, we're out the door.

"I'm overreacting, right?" glancing over at him.

"I'd rather be safe than sorry."

My eyes close as the back of my head hits the seat. One arm out the window as his hand rests on my thigh.

The breeze makes my shoulders drop an inch. The streets are packed with people as we make our way to Cassi's apartment. Pulling up in front, the tension returns to my neck in full force. The elevator button lights up as Ghost attempts to keep up.

Stepping in as the elevator doors open, elevator music assaults our ears. The ding interrupts the torture. My eyes narrow in on her door.

Okay, nothing's wrong so far.

The feeling of Ghost behind me relaxes me ever so slightly. Sensing my hesitation, he raises his fist and bangs on the door. Shuffling sounds from the inside as the door swings open to expose a shirtless, wide-eyed Ace standing in the doorway.

Sharing a look when Cassi's voice travels outside, "Come back to bed!"

Would you look at that?

SHADOWS AND DECEPTION

Acknowledgments

Thank you all so much for reading. I truly fell in love with these characters while writing them and hope you felt the same while reading. I would like to thank the man that has helped me fight my own demons.

If you would like to see more, please let me know at www.cjmckinney.com.

About the Author

CJ McKinney is an author who grew up in the beautiful mountains of Tennessee. She draws inspiration from the beauty that surrounds her— just like her two dogs, who ensure every writing session is filled with joy (and the occasional bark). Always an introvert, she is known to have her nose in a book no matter the occasion. The chaos in her mind intertwined with a true hopeless romantic creates a tale you'll never forget.

www.cjmckinney.com